BAYARD RUSTIN

BEHIND THE SCENES OF THE CIVIL RIGHTS MOVEMENT

JAMES HASKINS

Hyperion Books for Children
New York

Dedication

To Bryan DeWayne Haskins

Printed in the United States of America.

First Edition

3   5   7   9   10   8   6   4   2

Library of Congress Cataloging-in-Publication Data

Haskins, James, (date)
Bayard Rustin : Behind the Scenes of the Civil Rights Movement / James Haskins.
p.   cm.
Includes bibliographical references and index.
Summary: A biography of Bayard Rustin, a skillful organizer behind
the scenes of the American civil rights movement whose ideas strongly
influenced Martin Luther King, Jr.
ISBN 0-7868-0168-9 (trade) — ISBN 0-7868-2140-X (lib. bdg.)
1. Rustin, Bayard, 1910–   —Juvenile literature.   2. Civil rights
workers—United States—Biography—Juvenile literature.   3. Afro-Americans—
Civil rights—Juvenile literature.   4. Civil rights movements—United
States—History—20th century—Juvenile literature.
[1. Rustin, Bayard, 1910–   2. Civil rights workers.
3. Afro-Americans—Biography.   4. Afro-Americans—Civil rights.]   I. Title.
E185.97.R93H37   1997
323'.092—dc20   [B]   96-1256

Contents

Acknowledgments

I am especially grateful to Walter Naegle and the Bayard Rustin Fund, Inc., and to Patricia A. Allen, for their help. A special thank-you to Kathy Benson.

CHAPTER ONE

GROWING UP QUAKER

In future centuries, when people look back on our time, they will mark the twentieth century in America as the time when the United States finally lived up to the creed on which it was founded. The writers of that creed had written lofty words asserting that "all men are created equal" and "endowed by their creator" with the rights of "life, liberty, and the pursuit of happiness." But for nearly two hundred years African Americans were not included in this creed. It took nearly a century for the nation to abolish slavery and declare that black people were citizens. It was almost one hundred years more before the nation passed laws *guaranteeing* them the rights of citizenship.

These laws were passed only after a long campaign for civil rights was waged by African Americans and their white supporters. It was largely a nonviolent campaign, one that appealed to the best instincts of Americans. The civil rights movement operated on the idea that the human conscience needed only to be awakened to injustice to spur it into action and right the wrongs of the world.

Of all the personalities in the civil rights movement, one of the most influential was a man whose name was never a household word—at least not in most households. Bayard (pronounced Buyard) Rustin worked behind the scenes for decades, involved in all the most important civil rights battles. Rustin was not a great orator, like Martin Luther King Jr. But his ideas strongly influenced King. He was not a leader of any of the major civil rights organizations. But he either worked for, or helped establish, most of them. Bayard Rustin was the most skillful organizer in the civil rights movement. In the twenty-odd years between the first student sit-ins in Chicago in 1942 and the passage of the Civil Rights and Voting Rights acts in 1964 and 1965, he had a hand in nearly every major event of the civil rights movement. And he personally organized the huge March on Washington in 1963 that was the catalyst for those crucial federal rights laws passed in the two following years.

Twenty years is a dot on the pages of history, and yet those years in the twentieth century saw a sea change in life for African Americans. Bayard Rustin is just as responsible for that change as are the more public leaders of the civil rights movement. The others were the "stars," but he was the stage manager.

Bayard Rustin was born on March 17, 1912, in the town of West Chester, Pennsylvania. He was raised by his grandparents, Janifer and Julia Davis Rustin, whom he called Pa and Ma.

Bayard's grandfather, Janifer Rustin, was a caterer who provided the meals at the local white country club, as well as banquets for special events at the club and for wealthy families in town. Among his best clients was the Ricci family, who owned a large ice company and sold a special brand of iced tea. The Ricci family was large as well as wealthy, with about ten children. When their house became too small for the growing family, the elder Ricci rented their former house to the Rustin family. "For them it was small," Bayard Rustin later recalled. "But for us it was a big, big house. It had about ten rooms."

Julia Rustin was a nurse who had helped organize the Black Nurses Society. In West Chester, she had established a day nursery for black children, set up in cooperation with Cheyney Teachers College, a Quaker-run college for blacks just outside West Chester. Julia Rustin was a Quaker herself. Her mother had been reared in a Quaker household and had passed on the Quaker beliefs and traditions to her daughter.

Although Julia Rustin was a member of the local black church, the Bethel African Methodist Episcopal Church (Bayard would later attend that church and sing in its choir), she maintained her Quaker beliefs and passed them on to her children and grandchildren. Bayard, the youngest child in the household, was influenced by Quaker teachings from the first.

The Quakers, more formally known as the Religious Society of Friends, began in England in the mid–seventeenth century. The society was founded by a man named George Fox, who believed that no priest or religious rite was necessary for communion between a soul and God. Fox said that the Holy Spirit supplied everyone's heart with an "inner light," and that everyone could receive understanding and guidance from that inner light.

In the early days of the society, its believers frequently shivered as they experienced the blessing of communion with God, and the term "Quaker" was originally one of derision. It stuck, and eventually became a common nickname for the Religious Society of Friends.

Many Quakers emigrated from England to North America in search of freedom to practice their beliefs. The colony of Pennsylvania was founded by Quakers, and to this day the state of Pennsylvania remains a Quaker stronghold.

Julia Rustin taught Bayard the basic Quaker beliefs: to do no violence to others and to respect all people. She taught him by example, in ways a child could easily understand.

Years later, Rustin would remember attending a community Christmas service when he was about eight. He was shocked to see the town drunk—a white man—arrive at the service, and he said so. Julia Rustin hushed him and said they would talk about it later. After they got home, Rustin recalled, "She chastised me, but in a very nice way, saying, 'You must not judge other people, because if, as you say, he is the town drunk and is no good, then it must have taken much more energy for him to have come [to the community service] than it did for us.' "[1]

Julia Rustin was kind to whites in spite of the fact that many whites regarded blacks as second-class citizens at best, less than human at worst. When asked once how she could be so dignified when she had seen so much discrimination in her life, she replied, "Oh, I decided long ago that I was not going to let people mistreat me, and in addition give me indigestion."[2] She was also a leader in the local branch of the National Association for the Advancement of Colored People (NAACP), a civil rights organization with an integrated membership.

The early years of the twentieth century were a time of great unrest in the South. Many who lived in the states that had comprised the former Confederacy could not forget that they had been vanquished by the Union in the Civil War. They blamed the former slaves for the war and resented the postwar Reconstruction period when many blacks could vote and even win local political office. When Reconstruction ended and federal troops were withdrawn from the former Confederacy, the Southern states quickly took steps to restore the old order. Through a series of laws, blacks were returned to a condition of virtual slavery and forced to work in agriculture, the backbone of the Southern economy.

Segregation was the law of the South. Blacks could not attend white schools, go to the public library, or ride in the same streetcars as whites. In the late 1890s, a black man named Homer Plessy sued the city of New Orleans, Louisiana, over segregation on its streetcars. The case went all the way to the United States Supreme Court, which ruled in 1899 that "separate but equal" accommodations were constitutional. Thus, the court gave its stamp of approval to segregation in America.

In the North most states had abolished slavery long before President Lincoln officially ended it. So in places like West Chester, Pennsylvania, segregation was much milder than it was in the South.

When Bayard Rustin was a child, the elementary schools in West Chester were segregated by race. Although the Rustins lived in an Italian neighborhood, and Bayard's best friend was a boy from across the street named Pascale Dubondo, Bayard attended an all-black grade school.

But the school was not rigidly segregated. Half the teachers were white. The music teacher, who came one day a week, was white; so was the athletic director of the West Chester school system, who also came to Bayard's Gay Street School once a week. The children in the early grades went to the public library for storytelling. Years later, Rustin recalled, "Those first eight years of my schooling . . . were in a segregated school, in that most of the pupils were black, but with so many outside activities in which whites were involved . . . I never thought about the school as being segregated."[3]

In fact, young Bayard Rustin's major problem in elementary school was that he was left-handed, and his teachers kept trying to force him to write and draw with his right hand. This was common at the time; most people believed that right-handedness was "normal," and that children should conform. His grandmother, however, soon put a stop to that. She insisted that if Bayard was more comfortable using his left hand, he should be allowed to do so. It was not the first time, and it would not be the last, that Julia Rustin supported her grandson's individuality.

At Gay Street School, Rustin had his first important lessons in black history from a teacher named Miss Helena Robinson. What struck young Bayard Rustin most about Miss Robinson's teachings was her refusal to dwell on negative things, her insistence on emphasizing positive things: "She taught us, in a creative and inclusive rather than exclusive way, the importance of knowing something about our background in history."[4]

Miss Robinson taught her students about slavery. But rather than concentrating on its horrors, she pointed out that some slaves managed to escape from slavery. While it was illegal for slaves to read and write, some slaves managed to learn anyway. Some white Quakers were even sent to jail for teaching their black maids to read and write. She taught them about the abolitionists, black and white, who worked to end slavery. She took them to Quaker homes in and around West Chester that had once served as stations on the Underground Railroad, the informal network of free blacks, religious whites, and abolitionists who helped escaping slaves make their way north to freedom.

The students in Miss Robinson's class learned about the slave Joseph Cinque, who had led a slave revolt on the Spanish ship *Amistad* bound for Cuba. The slaves had risen up and taken over the ship, commanding its crew to return them to Africa. But the sailors then outwitted the slaves and headed instead for North America, where the *Amistad* ran aground off Long Island. Taken to Boston, Cinque and his men were the subjects of a court case between Spain and the United States. Spain wanted the slaves returned. The slaves, represented by former president John Quincy Adams, wanted to be free. In the end the slaves prevailed and were returned to Africa. "Poor Cinque didn't learn very much from his experience," Rustin commented as an adult, "because he went back to Africa and started a slave trade of his own."[5]

Rustin later recalled that Miss Robinson "was very careful to see that we got a picture in which all whites were not looked upon as monsters or blacks looked upon as all fine people . . . In other words, she taught me scholarship, that if you were going to look at a thing like slavery, look at the whole of it."[6]

Young Bayard Rustin also got an education in history outside of school. In the summers, Julia Rustin taught morning Bible classes in a small park in the black area of town. She and her pupils sat in the shade of a big tree, and she read to them from the Bible. She emphasized the Old Testament because, according to Rustin, "she was thoroughly convinced that we as black people had much to learn from the Jewish experience."[7]

There were very few Jews in West Chester, but the Bible was a good teacher. Bayard learned that the Jews had been forced to leave their homeland and were discriminated against in many lands where they tried to settle. Through these Bible classes, he learned that black people were not the only people in history to suffer.

Bayard and his family, while not rich, were never hungry. They always had clothes and shoes to wear and a roof over their heads. He learned firsthand about the suffering of poor black people by observing the black migrants from the South who stayed in the Rustin home on their way north.

After World War I there was a huge migration of blacks from the South to the North. One big reason was the mechanization of agriculture. Black labor, so important to Southern agriculture for centuries, was being replaced by farm machines. Poor Southern blacks were forced to move north in search of work. Blacks from states like Alabama and Louisiana usually headed for Detroit and Chicago. Those from Georgia, Florida, and South Carolina headed for New York.

Often they had little more than the clothes on their bodies; they certainly had no money for train fare. So they walked, sleeping in the fields beside the roads at night. Sometimes they found day work and earned a little money to take the train a little farther north. Frequently they depended on people of goodwill—black and white—and on black church congregations to help them.

The Rustin family welcomed migrants and gave them shelter. Often the boys would be hustled out of their beds late at night to make room for weary travelers. In the morning, the temporary guests would share breakfast with the family. Young Bayard was struck by their poverty and how they marveled at household conveniences he took for granted, like indoor plumbing and running water.

One night Bayard was awakened by the sound of moaning from the migrant family in the room next door. Then he smelled gas. He ran downstairs to awaken the adults in his family, and everyone ran from the house. Everyone, that is, except the migrant family. They had been overcome by the fumes. "These poor people from the South had been used to just taking the shade off the oil lamp and blowing out the flame before they went to bed," he explained years later. "They didn't understand that with a gas lamp, you had to turn the gas off. It was for me a very traumatic experience, and I think one of my earliest interests in trying to recognize the need to help people and to be concerned about people sprang from that unfortunate experience, because some of them were in the hospital two or three days before they could be released. Fortunately nobody died, but some of the younger children were in very serious trouble."[8]

Largely because of the activities of Julia Rustin, the Rustin household also played host to important and sophisticated black people. W. E. B. Du Bois, the first African American to earn a doctoral degree from Harvard and one of the founders of the NAACP, would stay with the Rustins whenever he was in town to deliver a lecture at the local college. So did Mary McLeod Bethune, the noted educator, and James Weldon Johnson, the renowned writer. Such people were educated, well traveled, and highly respected. Although they could afford to stay in a hotel, there were no hotels for blacks, and white hotels would not admit them.

Bayard Rustin was raised to treat all people the same—with kindness. But on one occasion he ignored the teachings of his family and went along with a gang of fifth-grade boys—all white except him—to the hand laundry operated by the one Chinese family in town. The boys threw open the door, tossed pebbles in, and began to chant, "Chink, Chink, Chinaman, eats dead rats, hit 'em in the head with a baseball bat."

"I cannot account for how it happened," Rustin later said, "because I knew it was wrong to do."[9]

He paid for his mistake. The Chinese man told Bayard's family, and as punishment Bayard was assigned to help out at the laundry after school for two solid weeks. But a worse punishment was his family's shame that he could have done such a thing. He never forgot it.

The following year, Bayard Rustin had another experience that he would remember all his life. He found out that the people he had always called Ma and Pa were not his parents, but his grandparents, and that the woman he thought was his older sister was really his mother.

"My mother was Florence Rustin," he explained many years later. "She was, I believe, about seventeen at the time of my birth, and my father, who was not married to her, was a young man around nineteen. They were both very immature youngsters. They had no way of taking care of me, and subsequently my grandparents, that is, my mother's mother and father, took me in."[10]

Bayard Rustin never elaborated on the circumstances surrounding his being told the real story, or how he felt when he learned his true parentage. He may have been told the truth after his mother, who had left town not long after he was born, returned with a new husband. Or perhaps his grandparents simply decided that, at age eleven or twelve, he was old enough to know the truth. But the news probably came as no major shock to him. It was not unusual for black parents to take in a daughter's illegitimate child and raise him or her as their own; and there was no terrible stigma about illegitimacy among most blacks. Whatever he felt, he accepted the truth and did not blame either his mother or his grandparents. As he said years later, "Until this day, I consider those relatives who are still living my brothers and sisters rather than my aunts and uncles."[11] And he considered Julia Rustin, his grandmother, the greatest influence on his life.

Among the things his grandmother did to try to prepare him for life as a black American was to discuss race relations with him. Bayard tried to understand what she was saying, but found it hard. For example, she would discuss the lynchings of blacks in the South with him; but nobody in his neighborhood ever got lynched.

Rustin recalled, "My grandmother never tried to keep these things from us; but she never tried to put too much on our backs so we couldn't carry it, either . . . I think I was probably in the fifth grade . . . and my grandmother was explaining what a lynching meant. I can remember saying to her [that] I'd heard [the word] *lynching*, but it never dawned on me what it really meant. And I said, 'Well, Mama, do people really do that sort of thing?' and she said, 'Yes, I'm afraid they do.' And I can remember going around asking some of the other children if they'd ever heard of lynching, and all of them had heard of it . . . But [when I] asked them, 'What does it mean? What is lynching? What happens when a man gets lynched?' they'd say, 'Well, he gets killed.' They had no idea, really, you know. And so I presume that the first I really had of any idea of the brutality of lynching, that it just wasn't like shooting a man or the like, was from her description."[12]

Bayard's grandmother would tell him that black men in the South were beaten for talking to a white woman; but nobody in his neighborhood ever got beaten for talking to a white woman. Ironically, it was not until Bayard Rustin, who had gone to a segregated elementary school, entered an integrated high school that he began to feel the sting of racism.

He wasn't discriminated against in school. He was well liked and very popular. But outside school, when he was with white friends, he was made to feel different. "When we went to the movies, I always had to sit over on a side where there were just two rows of seats running the whole length of the theater, and they could sit where they wanted . . . Or when we went into the five-and-ten at lunchtime, and I would see white kids sitting at the [lunch] counter, but if I went to the counter for something, they wanted me to pack it up and take it out."[13]

Rustin, a talented musician and singer, was also a fine athlete. He was involved in many sports in high school, including track and football. But in winter, when the teams went to the YMCA for extra practice, he could not go with them.

The discrimination he suffered because he was black affected his friendships with whites. One of his best friends was Jean Cessna, of French descent. Jean Cessna lived with an elderly aunt, who would not allow Bayard in their house. The boys were welcome in the Rustin home, of course, but Jean was afraid that his aunt wouldn't approve. So the two boys met every evening after dinner at the West Chester public library and stayed there until the library closed.

Both were on the track team. When Jean learned that Bayard could not go to the YMCA to practice in the winter, he decided to demand an explanation from the Y's director. "Therefore," Rustin recalled years later, "I think the first direct protest [against discrimination] that I ever saw was not on the part of a black, but on the part of Jean Cessna, who sat in on [refused to leave the office of] the director of the YMCA until he would at least come out and give me an explanation. [The director] was so bloody embarrassed that when I walked in, the man asked to be excused, and I did not have any idea until he came back, and I saw how red his eyes were, that he was so sensitive to have to explain this to me that he'd gone out and cried."[14]

Bayard understood that not just black people were discriminated against in West Chester. The Italian people, too, were looked down upon by other whites, not only because they were immigrants, but also because they were Catholics. In 1928, when Bayard was sixteen,

Governor Al Smith of New York State, a Catholic, ran for the Democratic presidential nomination. Religion was very much an issue in the campaign. Many Italians in West Chester supported Smith because they wanted to see a Catholic elected president of the United States. But the white Protestants in West Chester and in much of the country voted against him for the same reason. The country was not yet ready for a Catholic president. Smith lost to Herbert Hoover in a landslide election.

While working on the Al Smith political campaign, Bayard Rustin also learned the depth of feeling against Jews in West Chester. One of his Jewish friends asked him to go to the local country club to hand out Al Smith campaign buttons and leaflets. Rustin later recalled that they were "terribly abused" at the club, whose membership was mostly Episcopalian and Baptist. "But what made me so aware of anti-Semitism was that wherein they simply looked on me as being under his tutelage, which in part I was, nobody spit at me, or spit on me or called me a bastard, but they did him. That was when I discovered that very often Jews were treated even worse than blacks."[15]

By the time Bayard Rustin graduated from high school and left West Chester to go to college, he was well prepared for the outside world. Thanks to his grandparents and a few special teachers, he had a strong sense of himself and his own abilities; because he had grown up in a multiethnic environment, he understood that prejudice came in many varieties.

CHAPTER TWO

COLLEGE AND COMMUNISM

Bayard Rustin did well in high school, not only academically and athletically but also musically and socially. In fact, he was named valedictorian of his class. However his family had no money to send him to college.

Fortunately, Bishop Wright of the African Methodist Episcopal Church in Philadelphia heard about Bayard and visited the Rustin family. He felt that Bayard should go to college, and he worked hard to secure a scholarship for him. Wilberforce University in Ohio came through with a musical scholarship, and the bishop raised another hundred dollars for Bayard's travel expenses and for his room and board at school.

Bayard had no trouble fitting in at the predominantly white university. He added his impressive tenor voice to both the college chorus and quartet and traveled all over the country representing Wilberforce.

At Wilberforce, Bayard Rustin also discovered that he was homosexual. He developed a close friendship with a student from California. At holiday vacations, the young man would go home with Rustin. "We never had any physical relationship but a very intense, friendly relationship. At that point, I knew exactly what was going on, but I did not feel that I could handle such a physical relation-ship," he recalled.[1] His family also knew what was going on and accepted Bayard's relationship with his fellow student. "It was never an encouragement," Rustin recalled years later, "but it was a recog-nition. So I never felt it necessary to do a great deal of pretending. And I never had feelings of guilt."[2] "I think," said Rustin, "that a fam-ily in which the members know and accept one's lifestyle is the most helpful factor for emotional stability . . . There was never any con-flict. And yet there was never any real discussion."[3]

Bayard soon grew unhappy at Wilberforce because he did not feel challenged academically; nor did he feel that the students as a whole were treated well. A special source of resentment among the students was the miserable quality of the food. In his second year at Wilberforce, Bayard organized a strike to protest the bad food. Years later he admitted that he should have known that he risked his schol-arship in organizing the protest. Sure enough, he was asked to leave. He transferred to Cheyney Teachers College near West Chester. But he soon grew bored there and again left before earning his degree.

He went next to New York City, to live with his sister—actually, his aunt—Bessie LeBon, in Harlem, and to attend City College.

Harlem was an exciting place for Rustin. He had never seen so many black people. His aunt lived in the Sugar Hill area, home to black doctors, lawyers, and ministers, as well as to successful musi-cians, writers, and artists. Bessie LeBon herself was an amateur painter. Rustin was introduced to Hall Johnson, leader of the Hall Johnson Choir and one of the most important black musicians of his time. Johnson had trained many black musicians and singers, and Rustin felt honored to be invited to his home, which was a meeting place for musicians and artists. Because Johnson was a homosexual who did not flaunt his sexual preferences, Rustin looked to him also as a role model. Through the musicians he met at Johnson's, Rustin was able to get singing jobs to help pay his expenses at City College (tuition was free). He worked for a while as part of the backup quartet for the folksinger Josh White, and he also worked for the singer Leadbelly. But his main focus in New York quickly became politics, for at City College Bayard discovered the Communist party.

At that time—the late 1930s—the student body at City College was predominantly first-generation Jewish and Italian and was a beehive of political activity. The Communist party had a strong following among the students. It was the most outspoken political organization advocating equal rights for everyone, including blacks. Rustin was first attracted by student activities on behalf of the Scottsboro Boys, nine young men and boys who had been arrested and charged with the rape of two white women in Alabama. There was little question in the minds of all but the most racist Southern whites that the Scottsboro Boys had been falsely accused; the case became a national scandal. Among the strongest defenders of the Scottsboro Boys was the American Communist party, which supplied not only money but also attorneys for the nine men and boys. At City College, various student organizations held rallies in support of the Scottsboro Boys and raised money for their legal defense. Among these student groups was one called the Young Communist League.

The Young Communist League (YCL) was an organization for students who believed in communism as it was practiced in the Soviet Union. There, communism was a totalitarian system of government in which the Communist party controlled all aspects of life. Rooted in the idea that the only way to ensure an even distribution of wealth among all citizens was for the state to control the means of production of goods, communism claimed to be a revolutionary system that was far superior to the capitalist system of the United States and Western Europe. Under capitalism, ownership of production is in private hands and the majority of citizens work for capitalist owners.

Communists claimed that the root cause of racism was capitalism and promised full equality for all—a promise that naturally appealed to Bayard Rustin.

The antiwar stance of the Communist party also attracted Rustin. Adolf Hitler had risen to power in Germany and was proclaiming his nation's superiority. There was talk of a coming war in Europe, and the YCL believed that the American president, Franklin Delano Roosevelt, was eager to involve the United States in it. The Communist party claimed that Roosevelt wanted to protect the capitalist economy of the United States at all costs, and that he believed going to war would help lift the nation out of the Great Depression in which it had been mired since the stock market crash of 1929. Rustin, a Quaker, was against violence in all forms, and certainly against war. He had not been at City College long before he joined the Young Communist League.

The primary aim of the YCL was to radicalize the students. The administration of City College had assigned each of the many student political groups an alcove in a large room in the main section of the campus. From its alcove, the YCL distributed leaflets and recordings by the famous black singer Paul Robeson. But the YCL did more than staff their assigned alcove. They worked to gain influence in all the major institutions on campus.

"We managed to take over the City College newspaper," Rustin recalled. "And we managed to control the student senate. We managed to control the budget for how money was to be spent amongst the various student organizations, and we began the propaganda against Roosevelt and the war, which we said was definitely coming and was going to be Roosevelt's fault . . ."[4]

To the YCL, the passage of a conscription law providing for young men to be drafted into the armed services was proof that the president expected the United States to be involved in war. Rustin remembered, "When the conscription bill came up, we composed a song:

> It was on a Saturday night
> And the stars were shining bright
> When they passed the conscription bill.
> And the people they did say,
> From many miles away,
> It's the president and his boys on
> Capitol Hill, of course.
> "Oh, I hate war,
> And so does Eleanor,*
> But we won't be safe till everybody's dead."

"There were several stanzas, and that became probably the most popular antiwar song prior to World War II."[5]

Soon young Bayard Rustin had his first experience with the Federal Bureau of Investigation (FBI), which had been investigating and trying to stop any so-called subversive activity against the government. Communist party activity, because it worked to promote a

---

*President Franklin Roosevelt's wife

radically different form of government, was considered subversive.

Informed by his aunt's neighbors that men in suits had been by asking questions about him, Rustin immediately knew that FBI agents were investigating him, hoping to make his life difficult by causing suspicion among his neighbors. He decided to confront the situation head-on.

Not long afterward, a man arrived to question Rustin personally. Rustin wasted little time. He knocked on the walls of his apartment, calling his neighbors on both sides out into the common hallway. Then he announced, "This is an FBI man. He's here to question me. I refuse to say anything to him. I will have no relationship with him whatsoever. You are free to tell him whatever you want, but I just want you to know who he is and what his purpose is."[6] The FBI agent was embarrassed and did not come around again.

Working with the YCL, Bayard Rustin learned that he had a particular skill for organizing and attending to details. He used those skills to establish chapters, called cells, of the YCL throughout the City University system. In 1939, at the request of the YCL, he organized a Committee Against Discrimination in the Armed Forces. He fully realized that the main reason that the Communists wanted such a committee organized was to make it more difficult for Roosevelt to mobilize for war. But he also believed that if the United States did go to war, its black soldiers should have equal rights with whites. With others, he made contact and worked with Communist elements in the newly formed umbrella labor organization Committee of Industrial Organizations (CIO, later called the Congress of Industrial Organizations). A small number of workers were especially receptive to the communist ideas of workers' rights and worker control over the means of production.

During this period, Rustin came into contact with A. Philip Randolph, president of the Brotherhood of Sleeping Car Porters (BSCP), the first African American trade union in the United States.

Asa Philip Randolph, born in Florida in 1889, was twenty-three years older than Rustin. A tall, light-complected man, he was a veteran of civil and labor rights causes. Arriving in Harlem in 1911, he too had attended City College.

Randolph and a friend named Chandler Owen founded a newspaper for black workers and started six political and trade unions between 1914 and 1920. Then in 1925, black railroad porters, who could not join any of the white trade unions, asked Randolph to help them start their own. He responded by forming the BSCP. But it took six years of combating prejudice in both the white and the black communities to get the union admitted to the American Federation of Labor (AFL), an otherwise all-white group of unions. And it took another three years before the Pullman Company, whose founder George Pullman had invented the railroad sleeping car, recognized the union in 1934.

Now for the first time there was an organized and effective union of African American workers. A. Philip Randolph became one of the most respected and powerful black leaders in the country. He had a built-in nationwide network for distribution of political thoughts and literature.

Rustin had read about Randolph long before he actually met him; when they first came face-to-face, Rustin was in awe of the older man. Rustin could not believe that such a great and busy man would find the time to see a mere student. But Randolph was gracious and put him immediately at ease. He was especially struck by the way Randolph welcomed him. The older man rose from his desk and shook hands, then asked his visitor to have a seat, indicating a chair and making a dusting motion, as if he were dusting off the chair for his visitor. As he came to know Randolph, Rustin realized that this unconscious, gracious gesture was Randolph's standard way of greeting visitors.

Rustin was struck also by Randolph's dignity. Well-educated and trained as a Shakespearean actor, Randolph spoke in clipped and measured tones, a way of speaking that almost automatically commanded respect. Rustin would later affect a similar way of speaking— an impressive, deliberate speaking style and a clipped British accent.

As Randolph and Rustin talked, they realized they were interested in many of the same causes and philosophies. Most fundamentally, both men agreed that the root of racism was economic and that the way to equality for blacks was through equal opportunities in the workplace.

They disagreed, however, on the efficacy of communism. According to Rustin, Randolph said to him, "I am sorry to know that you are associated with Communists because I think you're going to discover that they are not really interested in civil rights. They are interested in utilizing civil rights for their own purposes."[7]

Randolph advocated socialism, an economic and political ideology midway between capitalism and communism. Socialism, like communism, favored collective or government control of the means of production and distribution of goods. But socialism was not totalitarian and allowed for more individual freedom.

As the United States appeared to gear up for war, one of Randolph's chief concerns was that black workers get an equal share of jobs in the defense industries. Blacks had suffered disproportionately during the Great Depression, and many were still unemployed.

Even so, Randolph knew that it would take pressure from the highest government sources to get the defense industries to hire them now. Thus he proposed a March on Washington to persuade President Roosevelt to order an end to discrimination in the factories that made war materials.

Randolph already had a network in place to spread the word among adults. But he wanted to reach young black people as well. He asked Bayard Rustin to establish a youth division for the March on Washington. There was no money to pay him, so Rustin simply added this task to his already full agenda when he attended meetings of various labor, black, and antiwar organizations.

More and more March on Washington committees sprang up around the country, and President Roosevelt decided not to risk a massive demonstration of blacks in the capital. One June 20, 1941, just two weeks before the scheduled march, he signed Executive Order 8802, banning discrimination in the war industries and establishing the Fair Employment Practices Commission. In turn, Randolph called off the march.

It is quite possible that had the march taken place, it would not have been very well attended. But many in the black community were angry with Randolph for calling it off. Rustin was among them. He was young and militant, and he believed that the march should have proceeded regardless. "We were crazy then," he recalled years later, remembering the frustration of black people, young and some old, who pleaded with Randolph, "'Even if you have that damned executive order, show your guts, man, march on Washington.'"[8]

In spite of his anger at the cancellation of the march, Rustin was impressed with Randolph's sense of honor and with the ultimate success of his threat to march in persuading the president to sign the executive order. Randolph, for his part, was impressed with Rustin's commitment to the cause of equal employment practices and with his organizational abilities. He asked him to work full-time for him, and Rustin accepted, knowing full well that he would not be paid a salary. Fortunately, his aunt Bessie believed in his work and was willing to support him.

By the time Rustin went to work for Randolph, he had broken with the YCL and rethought his previous commitment to communism. He had been disturbed by Russia's invasion of Finland in late November 1939. Russia had signed a nonaggression pact with Finland in 1934, and Rustin felt it should not have reneged on that pact.

Another reason for the break was that the American Communist party had ceased actively supporting the case of the Scottsboro Boys, thereby seeming to retreat from its commitment to racial justice. Recalled Rustin, "That's when I began to smell [that] there was something radically wrong."[9]

His final disillusionment with communism came just after Hitler's forces invaded the Soviet Union on June 22, 1941. The American Communist party was told to reverse its position on the war; it was now a "people's war," and the Communist party supported the war effort. The American Communist party's interest in racial equality was now less important than its support for the Soviet Union. Rustin was called in and asked to return in three days with a plan to dissolve the Committee Against Discrimination in the Armed Forces, which he had created. He realized that the party had already made its final decision to dissolve the committee; he was just being "let down easy."

When he returned three days later and announced that he refused to do what he had been asked, he was alternately threatened and cajoled. "They would see that I was taken off this committee at City [College], that I would lose my position on the newspaper, all this sort of thing. When they saw that didn't work, then they tried to butter me up by telling me how important I was and that I was going to be a great black leader someday, and I needed the training, and that I was momentarily confused . . . and I simply said no, that I couldn't do it. And I walked out."[10]

The work Rustin did next, and for the rest of his life, was based very much on what he had begun to learn at City College—not from his course work, but from his work with the YCL. As he said, "One of the reasons that I did not really do much studying those two and a half years I was at City College was that I was organizing all over the state of New York for the Young Communist League. I learned many of the most important things about organization and clearing [up] detail[s] and writing clearly and the like from my experience as a Communist."[11]

CHAPTER THREE

CONSCIENTIOUS OBJECTOR

By the time he left the Young Communist League, Bayard Rustin had made an important career choice. Although he continued to love music—besides performing at Cafe Society with folksinger Josh White, he had appeared in the 1940 Broadway production of *John Henry*, starring Paul Robeson—he found political work more exciting. At City College, it seemed to him that he had learned much more through his political activities than in class. He read widely on racism, classism, and economics. He talked frequently with A. Philip Randolph. He learned the fine points of organizing. But he never earned a college degree. In 1941, he left City College and went to work for the Fellowship of Reconciliation (FOR) as its youth secretary. That was the beginning of a professional career that would never assure steady, salaried employment, insurance benefits, or a retirement nest egg. Bayard Rustin would always take jobs because of principle, not material comfort or job security.

The FOR at that time was an interdenominational pacifist Christian group (later, a nonsectarian religious organization) that, unlike the Communist party, remained committed to the cause of black civil rights, despite its concern that the United States would soon enter World War II. Rustin's Quaker background and active interest in black equality made him a good match with the FOR, and he traveled extensively on the organization's behalf.

He distinguished himself early on as different from the average speaker because he often interspersed his remarks with spirituals and other songs from the African American experience, such as work songs and field hollers.

Rustin also wrote and produced a pamphlet for the FOR, entitled "Interracial Primer," which outlined some of the ways whites could help advance the cause of black equality.

One was to address blacks with respect. Racist whites, as well as many thoughtless whites, were in the habit of calling black people by their first names. They would never call a man named Thomas Jefferson "Mr. Jefferson"; instead they'd call him "Tom," or sometimes "Jefferson."

However, if a black man called a white man anything other than "Mr. So-and-so," he risked being beaten or killed for showing such a lack of respect.

In his pamphlet, Bayard Rustin wrote, "You can refer to blacks as Mr. Jones instead of Jones or Tom."

Another suggestion in the pamphlet was that white newspaper reporters pay equal attention to the race of accused criminals. At that time, when crimes were reported, accused white criminals were never identified by race, while those who were black always were. A news story about the arrest of a white man might say, "Arrested was Thomas Jefferson, thirty-six years old." A news story about the arrest of a black man would say, "Arrested was Thomas Jefferson, Negro, thirty-six years old." That kind of discrimination rankled with blacks. Wrote Rustin in his pamphlet, "It would be very important not to identify all criminal activity on the part of black people as 'So-and-so, black,' whereas you don't also say, 'So-and-so, white, did this crime.' "

Some forty-five years later, Rustin laughed at how his "revolutionary" suggestions seemed so naive to people of the 1980s, both black and white: "I showed the pamphlet to a group of high school students once, and they said, 'Well, why did you write this? What was this for?' "[1] They could not imagine a time when such basic respect was not accorded to African Americans.

While with the Fellowship of Reconciliation, Rustin helped form a new civil rights organization, the Committee on Racial Equality (CORE). Later called the Congress of Racial Equality, the organization was founded with the assistance and funding of the FOR but was not formally associated with it. Because the FOR was concerned with pacifist (nonviolent and antiwar) causes, it could not be true to its intent and philosophy and still sponsor the more confrontational actions that CORE was engaged in.

James Farmer, the young race relations secretary of the FOR, had joined that organization in 1941, the same year as Rustin, and had recently graduated from Howard University with a degree in theology. He was the one who first approached the FOR with the idea of founding an organization that would fight racial discrimination using the same techniques that Mohandas K. Gandhi was using in India.

Under the leadership of Mohandas K. Gandhi, called the Mahatma, or Great Soul, by his followers, nonviolent protest to bring about social change was achieving positive results in India. Indians of all castes, or classes, had united to secure their independence from Great Britain. Beginning in 1915, Indians followed Gandhi's philosophy of nonviolence, protesting against unfair British laws but not defending themselves when they were beaten, arrested, or jailed. The jails of India were filled to overflowing, but this only served to attract more Indians to the cause. It took many long years, but Gandhi's "soul force" eventually won out, leading Britain at last to surrender India to the Indians in 1947.

Although the FOR decided against sponsoring CORE directly, Farmer was authorized to establish the new organization while he continued to work for the FOR. In 1942, under the leadership of Farmer, Rustin, and several others, CORE offically came into being at the University of Chicago.

CORE's purpose was to confront racial injustice wherever it was found, taking a more confrontational approach than that of older civil rights organizations such as the NAACP and the National Urban League. Years later, Farmer recalled that an official of the Chicago Urban League described the differences among the organizations this way: "The Urban League is the State Department of civil rights; the NAACP is the War Department; and CORE is the Marines."[2]

One of CORE's first actions was to integrate Jack Spratt, a restaurant near the University of Chicago that did not serve blacks. First, the organization sent letters to the management of the restaurant requesting negotiations. When a team of two women students, one black and one white, went to the restaurant to talk about the issue, they were told that integration would be bad for business. The students suggested the restaurant try integration for a week or two to see if indeed there was a difference in its profits, but management refused. Late in the afternoon, three days later, twenty-eight CORE members and sympathizers undertook the first organized civil rights sit-in in American history. They entered the restaurant in groups of two, three, and four, with one black man or woman in each party, and occupied all the available seats. The restaurant personnel refused to serve them. The groups continued to sit where they were.

The restaurant management called the police and complained that the sitters-in were disturbing the peace. But James Farmer had notified the local police precinct about what CORE intended to do, and when two policemen arrived, they informed the management that there was no disturbance of the peace and quickly left. In the meantime, many white diners had stopped eating in support of the sit-in. The restaurant management, realizing they had no recourse, served the demonstrators. In a few short hours CORE had succeeded in integrating Jack Spratt. Integrated test groups, visiting the restaurant periodically over the next few weeks, reported no trouble.

The members of the young organization, elated by their victory, vowed to continue to fight injustice with such protests.

For the next few years, CORE continued to use nonviolent tactics to achieve integration, mostly on a small, local scale.

Rustin might have devoted more of his time to establishing and building the membership of CORE if he hadn't gone to jail for refusing to serve in the United States armed forces.

In December 1941, following the Japanese bombing of the U.S. naval base at Pearl Harbor, Hawaii, the United States had declared war on both Japan and Germany and had entered World War II on the Pacific and European fronts. America had already been sending supplies to England, France, and other nations arrayed against the forces of Adolf Hitler and Nazi Germany for two years, but until then had not actually entered the fighting. In order to wage war on both fronts, the United States needed a huge number of troops. While the draft, or call-up, of men who were eligible to fight had been instituted earlier, many more men were now called.

By law, members of three historic peace churches—the Mennonites, Brethren, and Quakers—were given gentle treatment if they applied for exemption from the draft based on their religion. They were called conscientious objectors, and if their applications were approved they were allowed to do alternative civilian service work. Such work could include working in hospitals, serving as guinea pigs for experimental medications, or fighting forest fires.

As a Quaker, a member of the Religious Society of Friends, Bayard Rustin was eligible for legal conscientious objector status. He certainly had the qualifications. Not only was he a Quaker, but he was a pacifist, opposed to war or violence as a means of resolving disputes. The following incident is a good illustration of how Rustin practiced pacifism.

During the war years, Rustin was riding on a train through Texas that was also carrying seven German prisoners of war guarded by military policemen (MPs). The MPs decided to have the Germans eat in the dining car before the rest of the passengers, and one American woman resented what she considered preferential treatment for the enemy. She slapped a German prisoner across the face.

Rustin witnessed this incident, and it offended his sense of fair play and brotherhood among all people. He tried to persuade the woman to apologize, but she would not. So he approached one of the MPs and asked for permission to speak to the Germans. The MP said it was against regulations for a civilian to speak to prisoners of war. Then Rustin asked, "Is there a regulation saying that I cannot sing to them?" The MP admitted that he knew of no such regulation. So Rustin sang a song by the Austrian composer Franz Schubert entitled "Serenade," and followed it with a song entitled "A Stranger in a Distant Land." Later, as the Germans passed by him, the one who had been slapped put his arm around Rustin's shoulder and said in halting English, "I thank you."[3]

Although Rustin could rightly apply for conscientious objector status, he did not feel it was fair to avoid the military draft in that way, since he had Methodist and Jewish friends who also considered themselves conscientious objectors but whose claims were not accepted. As he explained, "Inasmuch as I could not see myself taking the privilege that went with being a Quaker while my friends were being forced to go to jail, I took the position that I had to stand with my friends. I refused to register. I refused to take the physical examination, and I was sentenced to prison for three years. So I spent most of 1943, 1944, and half of 1945 in federal penitentiary[s]."[4]

For a young man as energetic as Bayard Rustin, one of the worst parts of being in prison was the sheer boredom of the routine. He took the opportunity to teach himself to play the lute, and that first lute was the beginning of a large collection of stringed instruments he would later acquire. Rustin also read every book he could find. And, being an organizer and a fighter against discrimination wherever and whenever it occurred, he soon found a way to engage in those activities even in prison.

Rustin was first sent to federal prison in Ashland, Kentucky, where the inmate population was primarily conscientious objectors and "moonshiners," convicted of brewing and selling illegal liquor. Among the one-hundred-odd conscientious objectors were members of the Jehovah's Witnesses, a sect whose members refused to fight in any war but Armageddon, the war they believed would occur at the end of the world. The majority of the prison population was white; the blacks were segregated. Bayard Rustin and the other conscientious objectors were opposed to segregation as a practice that did violence to men's souls. They formed a committee against segregation in the prison dining hall and elected Rustin chairman. Toward the end of 1943, the conscientious objectors launched a series of demonstrations. After three months they were successful and the prison was integrated.

Fresh from that victory, they launched another protest, this time against the censorship of books. Prison officials controlled the types of books, magazines, and newspapers available to the prisoners, and the prisoners believed they had a right to obtain any reading material they wanted. A group pledged to fast, or go without food, for as long as it took to end censorship. Twenty-two days later, the prison warden announced that censorship of books would be ended. That same day, Rustin and two other ringleaders of the two protests were handcuffed and transported to a federal prison in Lewisburg, Pennsylvania.

At Lewisburg, Rustin and about a dozen other "troublemakers" were confined to the library. "In other words," Rustin recalled, "they had simply washed their hands of us and said, 'Give them what they want. Keep them in one room. We don't want them infecting the population with their liberal ideas.'"[5] For the remainder of his time in prison, Rustin and his associates were able to read whatever books they wanted. Their meals were brought into the library. The only times they left the library were to take showers and exercise, and at those times other prisoners were not at the showers or in the exercise yard. There was little point in protesting, and protests were few, short, and mild.

In May 1945, the United States and its European allies won the war in Europe against Nazi Germany and its allies. The war in the Pacific, against Japan, dragged on for several more months. In

August 1945, the United States dropped atomic bombs on Hiroshima and Nagasaki, Japan, and the war quickly ended.

The bombs leveled the two cities and killed or maimed thousands of ordinary Japanese citizens. Bayard Rustin was appalled at this mass destruction of life. While he understood that U.S. President Harry S. Truman had ordered the bombings because he believed they would bring about the end of the war and prevent the loss of more American lives, in his view nothing could justify the wholesale destruction that the bombs had wreaked. After his release from prison, he conducted workshops and lectured against the use of atomic weapons and added his name to petitions asking the nations of the world not to develop or test atomic weapons. He also engaged in demonstrations, including one in France against French testing of atomic weapons in the Sahara Desert in the early 1960s.

Rustin was released from prison a couple of months after the war ended. He realized that the prison system wanted only to get rid of him and the other "troublemakers"; but he didn't care what the reason was. As soon as he could do so, he went to West Chester, Pennsylvania, to visit his family. Sadly, his grandfather had died while he was in prison. Had Rustin chosen to do noncombat war service, an option that had been available to him as a conscientious objector, he might have been free to visit his grandfather before he died, or at least to attend the funeral and share in his family's mourning. But he accepted the consequences of having made the choice to go to prison for his beliefs.

He understood that his prison experience was much different from that of most other inmates, for he was there by choice, and on principle. "Not necessarily that we were right," he explained years later, "but that we thought we were right, and we thought, therefore, that we were making a contribution to society in the same way that Mahatma Gandhi, who was our hero, had said to the British judge when he had come before him, 'It is your moral duty to put me in jail. And you are not doing your duty if you don't jail me.' And that was our feeling, because we felt that it was by going to jail that we called the people's attention to the horrors of war."[6]

Rustin also knew that his prison experience was different from that of the average prisoner because he had influential friends in the outside world—religious groups, groups concerned with civil liberties—who watched out for him. A. J. Muste, who headed the FOR, frequently visited the conscientious objectors who were members of the FOR. A. Philip Randolph sent messages to Rustin through Muste. But in some ways prison was just as difficult for Rustin as it was for criminals, because "one is unable to be a human being in that one is never able to make a single decision about anything that he thinks is important."[7] He cannot decide when to eat, when to shower, when to turn his light on or off, when to exercise, when not to exercise. "That robs people of their inner capacity to be a human being and almost all of the violence [in prison] springs from that."[8]

Not long after his release, Rustin talked with A. Philip Randolph about his prison experience. Randolph suggested that he spend a year going to universities, colleges, women's groups, and anywhere else where he could be heard, to talk about his prison experience. The American Friends Services Committee, a Quaker organization, had a speakers bureau, and Rustin traveled and spoke widely under its auspices.

He also traveled widely organizing antisegregation demonstrations, including in the South, where it was the most dangerous to do so. Rustin, however, was never in serious fear for his life. As he explained, he always tried to appeal to the best instincts of white Southerners, and often found that their instincts were more humane than those of Northerners: "I would say to the manager [of a hotel or restaurant or theater], 'Look, I try to be a human being . . . We are human beings together . . . I don't think you're the type who wants to call somebody a nigger or keep them out . . .' [I can't count] the number of times that Southerners said things to me that Northerners never said, such as, 'Mr. Rustin, I wish you could get some kind of a law passed, because if you really got a law passed I'd have an excuse for serving you. But I don't want to lose all my business. If I could tell people it's a law, I'm sure they'd want to abide by it.' That argument I seldom got from Northerners. Very interesting psychologically."⁹

CHAPTER FOUR

GREATER MILITANCY

In 1946, Rustin was asked by the FOR to organize a Free India Committee to support the Indian independence movement. Rustin was pleased to do so because, like others in the FOR and across the United States, he was impressed by the philosophy and tactics of nonviolent social protest as represented in the work of Mohandas K. Gandhi.

Like A. Philip Randolph, Gandhi believed that the key to independence was economic power. Only a small proportion of the Indian population was well-off; the majority lived in grinding poverty. The differences in economic class were reflected in the strict social lines drawn in Indian society, which was organized into castes. Gandhi believed that every Indian should be able to provide for his everyday needs himself. He set an example by growing his own food and by keeping his needs to a minimum. He even went about in a loincloth and sandals to demonstrate that a man trained as a lawyer in England and belonging to one of the upper castes in Indian society considered himself no better than the most wretched "untouchable," an individual so low in Indian society that he was beneath the caste system.

Gandhi's first major protest against the British who ruled India had been an economic one. The British government in India had a monopoly on salt; it was against the law for anyone else to make salt. On March 12, 1930, Gandhi announced that he would march fifty miles to the sea, where he would make salt. Thousands of Indians joined the march. Many were beaten. As soon as Gandhi started to make salt, he was arrested and jailed.

His demonstration sparked the imagination of other Indians, who began calling Gandhi the Mahatma, or Great Soul, and in a few years many were being arrested and jailed for noncooperation with the government. Before long, going to jail was a matter of pride for most Indians. Although there were occasional breakdowns in discipline, on the whole the Indian people followed Gandhi's advice that the best weapon against the British was the "soul force" (called *satyagraha*) of moral right.

By the time Bayard Rustin formed the Free India Committee, world opinion was strongly on the side of the Indians, and the Indian independence movement was close to success. Just one year later, in 1947, Britain signed a treaty granting India the right to determine its own destiny.

But inside India, there were clashes between the two major religious groups, Hindus and Muslims, and on January 30, 1948, a Hindu fanatic shot and killed Gandhi. The nation and the world were deprived of the soul force that had been the best hope for peace.

Sadly, Bayard Rustin never got to meet Gandhi. He did not reach India until 1949, the year following the assassination. He went to India to attend a conference that had been called by Gandhi before his death and that was, subsequently, dedicated to his memory. While there, Rustin became acquainted with one of Gandhi's sons, Devadas, as well as with Jawaharlal Nehru, a longtime fighter for independence and a follower of Gandhi's, who became the first prime minister of free India.

It may have been while in India that Rustin added to his collection of antique stringed instruments, such as lutes, harpsichords, violas, and guitars. By the 1950s, he had amassed a substantial collection, primarily by visiting antique shops and flea markets in New York and elsewhere in the United States, but also during his travels abroad.

Returning to the United States from India, Rustin was more convinced than ever that the tactics of nonviolent protest could work in the fight for racial equality. He persuaded the leaders of CORE that it was time to try the strategy of nonviolence on a larger scale than simply sitting in at lunch counters.

One of the most maddening indignities that black Americans had to suffer was segregation on transportation. In most areas of the South, there was separate seating on buses and separate cars on trains. A black person traveling from a state where there was no segregation to a state where there was had to change seats, or cars, when the vehicle crossed state lines. On June 3, 1946, the United States Supreme Court ruled in the case of *Morgan v.* [versus] *Virginia* that segregation of passengers crossing state lines was an "undue burden on interstate commerce." Interstate travelers should be exempt from segregation. While the decision affected only one small aspect of the overall pattern of segregation in the American South, it was nevertheless significant, for it was the first time that any national statement was made that it was wrong to segregate.

CORE was keenly aware of the ruling's significance. CORE had been growing more and more independent of the FOR. During World War II, many of the blacks working in CORE and participating in its direct-action efforts did not want CORE associated with a pacifist organization that didn't support the United States's entry into the war. Nevertheless, the FOR had continued to pay Rustin's salary as field director of CORE, as he traveled all over the country organizing demonstrations and sit-ins in segregated restaurants, hotels, theaters, and barbershops. When CORE wanted to do something to test the Supreme Court's *Morgan* decision, the Racial-Industrial Committee of the Fellowship of Reconciliation agreed to sponsor a "Journey of Reconciliation." Sixteen volunteers, all men, both black and white, would travel through the upper South to see whether these states were complying with the Supreme Court ruling. The blacks included a student, an attorney, a musician, and a church social worker. The whites included a printer, a biologist, two Methodist ministers, and the editor of the Workers Defense League *News Bulletin*. They traveled on Greyhound and Trailways buses during a three-week period, from April 2 to 23, 1947. Rustin kept a diary the whole time, in order to make a full report at the end.

The journeyers started out from Washington, D.C., and traveled through Virginia, North Carolina, Tennessee, and Kentucky. On some legs of the trip, the blacks sat in the front, and the whites in the back. On other legs, integrated groups sat together.

They encountered a variety of reactions from bus drivers and passengers, black and white. Some bus drivers were hostile; others apologized for having to call the police. Some white passengers gave their names and addresses to the journeyers, in case they needed support in court. Some black passengers angrily called the journeyers crazy or pleaded with them to move. Virginians, whose state had been the defendant in the *Morgan* case, were familiar with the Supreme Court ruling, and there were few incidents there—although in Petersburg, one of the black volunteers was arrested for sitting in the second seat from the front. This was on a Trailways bus; all the arrests of journeyers took place on Trailways buses, none on Greyhounds. As soon as it had become evident that interracial groups were testing compliance with the Supreme Court ruling on interstate transportation, the management of Greyhound had issued orders to let the groups ride. The management of Trailways had issued opposite orders.

The only violence occurred in Chapel Hill, North Carolina. One white and one black journeyer were arrested for sitting up front together. Sensing that the other passengers were sympathetic, Rustin and Igal Roodenko, the white printer, moved up to take the seats the other two had vacated. They, too, were arrested. The bus was delayed nearly two hours. White taxi drivers standing around the bus station were incensed, and one punched James Peck, the white editor of the Workers Defense League *News Bulletin*. Peck did not respond.

In his report on the Journey of Reconciliation, Rustin drew a number of conclusions. One was that the best word to describe the attitude of police, passengers, and riders of both races was "confusion." Another was that more such direct-action tactics must be undertaken by individuals and groups. "We are equally certain," he added, "that such direct action must be nonviolent."[1]

The Journey of Reconciliation was very risky for its time. Never before had an integrated group traveled even through the upper South to test compliance with antisegregation laws. There had been little violence, and comparatively few arrests. But the unpleasantness that had occurred on the Trailways buses had caused the CORE and FOR leaderships to abandon the journey on that line.

Furthermore, there was such fear on the part of local black officials that the journeyers who had been arrested, and who had expected to mount a successful legal challenge based on the Supreme Court decision, ended up serving time on Southern chain gangs.

Rustin and his friend Roodenko had been arrested in Chapel Hill, North Carolina. They were promised representation by lawyers for the NAACP, and they expected to plead not guilty and avoid prison. But two days before they were to return to that city for trial, Roy Wilkins, head of the NAACP, called Rustin with some bad news.

"You've got to go on the chain gang, because we are not going to make a case," Wilkins said. "We are going to ask you to plead guilty." When Rustin asked why, Wilkins explained that the local black attorney whom the NAACP expected to represent the journeyers claimed he had lost the stubs of the tickets proving that they were interstate passengers. Everyone knew that the real story was that he had been paid off by local whites to lose the stubs.

Explaining how a black attorney could have betrayed the journeyers, Rustin later said, "This was a period similar to that in South Africa today, where for every black who was a resister there were two or three blacks in every community who, because of fear or poverty or miseducation or cowardice—or for money—were prepared to be spies."[2] Without proof, Rustin and Roodenko had no case.

Several trials were held to decide the fate of the journeyers who had been arrested. In both cases in which an interracial team had been arrested, judges gave the white members harsher sentences. Rustin recalled years later that when he and the three others who had been arrested in Chapel Hill—Andrew S. Johnson, Joseph A. Felmet, and Igal Roodenko—came before Judge Chester A. Morris in Hillsboro, North Carolina, the judge told Rustin, "Well, I know you're a poor, misled nigra from the North. Therefore, I'm going to give you thirty days on the chain gang." Then the judge turned angrily to the timid horticulturalist Igal Roodenko. "Mr. Rodenky," he said, purposely mispronouncing Roodenko's name, "I presume you're Jewish, Mr. Rodenky. It's about time you white Jews from New York learned that you can't come down here bringing your nigras with you to upset the customs of the South. Now, just to teach you a lesson, I gave your black boy thirty days on the chain gang, now I give you ninety."

Years later, Rustin would joke to his friend, "Well, you see, there are some advantages to being black," and Roodenko would laugh.[3]

The other white, Joseph Felmet, was also sentenced to a chain gang. All three appealed their sentences, and their cases were tied up in the courts for two years.

Rustin, free pending his appeal, returned to his work for CORE, the FOR, and A. Philip Randolph. One of the many causes on which Randolph was focusing at that time was an end to discrimination and segregation in the armed forces. Since the end of the war, Randolph and others had been pressuring President Harry S. Truman to issue an executive order banning racial discrimination in the military. Randolph had formed a Committee Against Discrimination in the Armed Forces and appointed Bayard Rustin as acting head of the committee's youth division. The effort eventually paid off, and Truman agreed to issue the executive order. Randolph, for his part, agreed to disband the committee.

Randolph called Rustin in, along with a committee member named William Sutherland, and explained to them that he intended to call a press conference for the following afternoon to announce his decision. Rustin and Sutherland argued against disbanding the committee. Why not build on the momentum to pressure the president to issue an executive order ending *all* discrimination in the United States? But Randolph was a man of honor, and he had promised to disband the committee once the president had agreed to his wishes.

Angrily, Rustin and Sutherland did Randolph's bidding and arranged a press conference for him the following afternoon. But in defiance they called a press conference of their own for the morning of the same day. At that morning press conference they announced, "Mr. Randolph at four o'clock this afternoon has called a press conference at which he is going to [disband] this committee. We want you to know that we are opposed to his turning it down, and we want to continue this fight far beyond the armed services. We want an executive order eliminating all discrimination in the United States."[4]

In those days, there were early-afternoon editions of many newspapers in New York City. By calling their press conference for the morning, Rustin and Sutherland scooped Randolph and made their point.

Recalled Rustin of his defiant act, "This experience of mine stood me in good stead later to understand Stokely Carmichael and Rap Brown [who in 1966 turned the Student Nonviolent Coordinating Committee toward greater militancy in defiance of more moderate civil rights leaders], because I, myself, had been as radical in a way in regard to Randolph as they were now being to Dr. Martin Luther King. Well, the thing that makes this worth telling is that obviously we, without Mr. Randolph's prestige, could not hold such a committee together. We were youngsters. But more important is the fact that it was two years before I dared see Mr. Randolph again, after having done such a terrible thing."[5]

During the time he was out of touch with Randolph, Rustin continued to work at projects of which Randolph would have approved. Besides working as a field secretary for CORE and for the FOR, he worked for the independence of African nations, which, like India, were ruled by European countries. He also served his time on the North Carolina chain gang.

After two years of litigation, Rustin's conviction following his arrest on the Journey of Reconciliation had been upheld by higher courts. When the Supreme Court of North Carolina also ruled against the journeyers, Rustin and the three others returned to North Carolina to do their time.

Rustin surrendered to the Orange County court at Hillsboro, North Carolina, on Monday, March 21, 1949, to begin serving his thirty-day sentence. "We were treated terribly," Rustin remembered years later. Prisoners were hung by their wrists, put in a hole in the ground and denied food and water, and subjected to other indignities. At one point, the guards ordered Rustin to dance, and when he refused, they began shooting their pistols at his feet. "Of course I wouldn't do it," he later explained, "which greatly embarrassed them because this created a feeling amongst the other prisoners that they did not always have to do what they were told to do."[6]

Rustin was an exceptional prisoner. He had influential friends on the outside, who checked up on him regularly. A poor, friendless black prisoner might easily have been killed for such insubordination. But Rustin's death would have raised too many questions and prompted an investigation into conditions on the chain gang. Still, on his release, Rustin made sure that such an investigation took place. During his twenty-two days on the North Carolina chain gang (he was let off early for good behavior), he took notes on his own experiences and those of fellow prisoners and had them smuggled out of the camp. After his return to New York, he wrote extensively about the inhuman conditions for prisoners on the gangs. His account was serialized in the *New York Post* and caused considerable debate about chain gangs. Within two years, chain gangs were abolished in North Carolina.

Thus, in retrospect, Rustin considered his time on the chain gang to have been time well spent. The same was true of the Journey of Reconciliation. He believed it was such nonviolent forms of protest that made later protests against segregation on public transit possible.

Following his stint in prison, where he'd had ample time to think, Rustin screwed up his courage and called for an appointment with A. Philip Randolph. Rustin had not dared to approach the older man in the two years since his unauthorized press conference to protest the disbanding of the Committee Against Discrimination in the Armed Forces. He knew that Randolph had been terribly upset about his and William Sutherland's earlier defiance and wondered if Randolph would speak to him. To his relief, Randolph agreed to see him the afternoon of the very day he called.

When Rustin entered Randolph's office, the older man immediately rose from his desk and came forward to meet him. "He shook my hand," Rustin recalled, "and I was so nervous I was shaking, waiting for his wrath to descend upon me." But Randolph was delighted to see him, exclaiming, "Bayard, where have you been? You know I have needed you!" Rustin was overwhelmed by Randolph's forgiveness and generosity of spirit. He said, "From that day until the day Mr. Randolph died, he never once said a word to me about the mistreatment that I had given him on that [earlier] occasion."[7]

CHAPTER FIVE

THE CIVIL RIGHTS MOVEMENT BEGINS

As the 1950s began, Bayard Rustin continued to be involved in the international arena, traveling to Africa to assist in various independence movements. His first trip was to Ghana, where he helped Kwame Nkrumah, later the first president of independent Ghana, organize the youth division of his political party. Nkrumah then recommended Rustin to Nnamdi Azikiwe, whose chain of newspapers in Nigeria was helping him build a strong power base there. Rustin spent a year in Nigeria helping Azikiwe edit *The Pilot*, his main national newspaper, and freeing Azikiwe to concentrate on his political work. In 1954, Azikiwe was elected premier of East Nigeria.

Back in the United States, Rustin helped to organize the Committee Against Apartheid in South Africa. He had become interested in the racial problems of South Africa through his study of the life of Gandhi, who had spent many years in that country before returning to his Indian homeland. Apartheid ("apartness" in Afrikaans, the language of white South Africans of Dutch descent) is a term used in South Africa to describe the legal separation of the races. The groundwork for the policy had been laid down by the British, who had practiced segregation against all nonwhite South Africans. But the official, Afrikaner-imposed system of rigid segregation known as apartheid began in South Africa in 1948, after Daniel Malan was elected the first prime minister from the Afrikaner Nationalist Party. It was legally instituted in the early 1950s with a series of acts governing every aspect of South African life. Apartheid was a far more stringent type of segregation than that which existed in the United States, with almost no rights for black South Africans and only limited rights for those of mixed race.

In 1952, the FOR helped establish the Committee Against Apartheid. As Rustin explained, it was important that the FOR, whose pacifist members had not been able to support World War II, take a strong position against injustice. The FOR did not expect to have a significant impact on the policies of the South African government. They hoped, however, that if the nonwhite South Africans knew that there was a committee of American supporters who believed in nonviolence, they themselves might be more inclined to fight apartheid with nonviolent means. The Committee Against Apartheid, founded by Rustin, James Farmer of CORE, and George Houser, a white member of the FOR who had been executive secretary of CORE during the 1947 Journey of Reconciliation, was the first committee in the United States whose purpose was to protest apartheid in South Africa.

Rustin's main activities continued to be in the United States, promoting nonviolent protest to secure civil rights. Working primarily for CORE and the FOR, he traveled across the northern half of the nation organizing conferences and leading demonstrations against segregation. In 1953 he was in Pasadena, California, organizing a series of marches and protests against discrimination in theaters, hotels, and restaurants, when he was arrested on a morals, or "sex perversion," charge—specifically for soliciting another man to engage in a homosexual act. Rustin was convinced the FBI had set him up in order to undermine the civil rights work he was doing. Found guilty on the morals charge, Rustin was sentenced to thirty days in prison, an experience he did not wish to relive, ever.

The whole psychology was different, he later explained, because in this case everyone knew he was in jail because he'd done something they did not approve of, whereas all the other times he had been (or would be) in prison, he was there on moral principle.

Far worse for him than the thirty days in prison were the repercussions within the FOR. He was promptly "released" from his duties with the FOR because they felt his arrest would hurt their cause. "It was amongst the Fellowship people that there was hypocrisy . . . it was there that I found some of the worst attitudes to gays . . . Many of the people in the Fellowship of Reconciliation were absolutely intolerant in their attitudes."[1]

Rustin worried about how his arrest might affect his other work in the civil rights and peace movements. He had always tried very hard not to allow his homosexuality to intrude on his work, knowing that it would be seized upon as a way to censure the work in which he believed.

After he served time in prison for his conviction on the morals charge, he attended a working party of the American Friends Services Committee, helping write a pamphlet about the relevance of pacifism in the modern world. He argued various points with brilliance and functioned as an important reconciler of disagreements among the writers. He had to leave a day early because of other commitments, and on the last day he explained that he had only one request: that his name not be listed among the authors of the booklet. The others protested, but he explained that he was gay and had been jailed on a morals charge; his name might hurt the sale of the booklet, which, he felt, was too important to be handicapped by his association. He then rose and sang "Nobody Knows the Trouble I've Seen," followed by "There Is a Balm in Gilead." The group was so moved that they could not respond, but Rustin simply said, "Dear friends, I am at peace. I ask you to leave my name off." They did.[2]

A. Philip Randolph also continued to be supportive of his younger associate. Rustin recalled, "Someone came to Mr. Randolph once and said, 'Do you know that Bayard Rustin is a homosexual? Do you know he has been arrested in California? I don't know how you could have anyone who is a homosexual working for you.' Mr. Randolph said, 'Well, well, if Bayard, a homosexual, is that talented— and I know the work he does for me—maybe I should be looking for somebody else homosexual who could be so useful.' Mr. Randolph was such a completely honest person he wanted everyone else also to be honest. Had anyone said to him, 'Mr. Randolph, do you think I should openly admit that I am homosexual?' his attitude, I am sure, would have been, 'Although such an admission may cause you problems, you will be happier in the long run.' Because his idea was that you have to be what you are."[3]

Although he was no longer working for the FOR, Rustin found plenty to do for CORE and for A. Philip Randolph. He had an unparalleled genius for organizing and an unwavering commitment to civil and human rights. As the direct-action civil rights movement of the 1950s and 60s began, his commitment and skills were greatly needed.

Again, it was the indignities of segregated travel that sparked the movement. This time it was segregation on the city buses of Montgomery, Alabama. Blacks not only had to sit in the rear seats, they also had to pay at the front and then get back off the bus and go around to the side door to board again. If the seats in front for whites filled up, blacks would have to give up their seats in the back to standing white passengers.

The first law to segregate blacks from whites on public transportation in Montgomery had been passed in the early years of the century, and black Montgomeryites had attempted to boycott public transportation at that time, without success. They had acquiesced to the indignities for years, until just after World War II, when many returning black soldiers protested strongly having to suffer discrimination back home in their own country after having risked their lives for their country in the war. In response, in 1945, Montgomery passed a new law aimed at making the old one even stronger.

The local branch of the NAACP was one of many organizations and individuals that had protested the new law, bringing petitions to the city and the bus company. Their protests went unanswered. So the NAACP decided that the best way to win equality was through the courts. In 1954, after decades of court cases, the NAACP had managed to bring the matter of segregated public schooling before the United States Supreme Court and to convince the nine justices that separate schools for blacks could never be equal to those of whites. In practice, having "separate but equal" schools simply didn't work. The Supreme Court decision in the case *Brown v. Board of Education, Topeka*, the NAACP and others believed, could be applied to other areas of life as well, including segregated transportation.

The Montgomery NAACP was headed by E. D. Nixon, who worked as a sleeping car porter and was the Southern representative of A. Philip Randolph's union, the BSCP. He had worked with Randolph in planning the aborted 1941 March on Washington. Although Nixon possessed only a grade-school education, he was smart, and he was determined to find a likely plaintiff to bring suit against the city of Montgomery and its bus company. Unfortunately, several possible plaintiffs proved unsuitable for one reason or another. Rosa Parks, a seamstress who served as secretary for the Montgomery NAACP, knew well that for a suit to be successful in court, the person who brought the suit had to be respectable and, ideally, a woman. While the continued search for a strong plaintiff was no doubt in the back of her mind when she boarded a city bus after work on the evening of Thursday, December 1, 1955, her immediate thoughts were on getting home and on the NAACP Youth League Christmas pageant she was organizing. Otherwise she never would have boarded that particular bus, for she was stunned to recognize the same driver who had put her off a bus twelve years before. Back in 1943, she had boarded a crowded bus at the front, rather than try to push through the people at the back. The driver, enraged, had put her off the bus. From that time on, whenever she recognized that particular driver, she chose to wait for the next bus.

Still, once on and having paid her fare, Parks could do nothing this evening but remain on the bus. She took a seat in the front row of the colored section. The bus grew more crowded, and when the driver noticed white people standing, he ordered the blacks in the first rows to give up their seats. Rosa Parks refused to move and was arrested for violating the segregation laws. The NAACP now had its perfect plaintiff: a forty-two-year-old woman, rather prim in her bun and spectacles, with a husband, a steady job, and no previous arrest record.

In fact, Rosa Parks was such an upstanding citizen that some black Montgomeryites chose not to wait for the NAACP to pursue her case in the courts. Led by JoAnn Robinson, a teacher at the all-black Alabama State University, a group of fed-up black people distributed a handbill calling for a bus boycott the following Monday. Local NAACP leaders saw to it that the handbill was printed in the *Montgomery Advertiser*, a newspaper. The ministers of local black churches devoted their sermons that Sunday to the indignities of bus segregation and urged their parishioners to observe the boycott.

The following Monday, December 5, 1955, the Montgomery city buses were practically empty, as black people walked to work, took cabs, or carpooled. Local black leaders were overjoyed—this was the first time ever that black citizens had joined together in massive protest of a segregation law. They vowed to continue the boycott until segregation on the city buses was ended.

Meanwhile, Mrs. Parks was found guilty, given a suspended sentence, and required to pay a small fine. The NAACP immediately filed an appeal, and over the next twelve months the case was heard in higher and still higher courts until finally it went all the way to the United States Supreme Court.

Just days into the boycott, local black leaders formed an organization called the Montgomery Improvement Association (MIA) to sustain the boycott. They held meetings, publicized the boycott, and raised money. E. D. Nixon decided that the young minister of the Dexter Avenue Baptist Church, Dr. Martin Luther King Jr., was the best person to head the new organization. King protested. At age twenty-seven, he felt he was too young to take on such a responsibility. Moreover, he was too new to Montgomery. But Nixon assured him that he was the best man for the job for just those reasons. Because he was so new in town, he had not had time to make either close friends or serious enemies. Nixon sought and secured a unanimous vote urging King to accept leadership of the MIA, and King reluctantly agreed to serve.

No sooner had King taken on his new responsibility than Lillian

D. Smith, a white Georgia writer who supported integration and who had written a book about lynching, called *Strange Fruit*, contacted Rustin. The two knew each other through the Fellowship of Reconciliation, on whose board she served, through CORE, with whose work she had been associated, and through their mutual interest in Gandhi's nonviolent movement in India. Smith considered Rustin, as he once put it, "a kind of minor authority on nonviolence,"[4] and telegraphed him to say he was needed in Montgomery. In her view, the bus boycott could succeed only if it adhered to the principles of nonviolence. She also sent a telegram to King informing him that she had asked for Rustin's help.

Black leaders in Montgomery were averse to having Rustin involved. They immediately contacted A. Philip Randolph to ask him to persuade Rustin not to go South. They agreed that Rustin had impeccable credentials in nonviolence, that he was a masterful organizer, and that his lyrical tenor voice would come in handy at church meetings where hymns and freedom songs were so important. But Rustin also had a lot against him.

First of all, he was a Northerner, and the boycott was a Southern movement. The organizers did not want the boycott criticized as being instigated by Northerners. Rustin later said that many also feared that his background as a former Communist, pacifist, conscientious objector, and homosexual was potentially hurtful to the movement. Still, Randolph believed, as did Rustin, that the success of the Montgomery bus boycott might lead to a larger nonviolent campaign for civil rights in the South, so it was especially important that the movement have the aid of a skilled organizer and tactician in nonviolence. Randolph raised the money to pay for Rustin's trip to Montgomery.

Rustin arrived in Montgomery on February 21, 1956, just after a state circuit court grand jury had handed down indictments against nearly one hundred members of the MIA for violating Alabama's antiboycott law. He suggested that those on the "wanted list" turn themselves in, following the Gandhian technique of "moral jujitsu." They did so and, by surrendering, seized the moral high ground. Going to jail for the cause became a badge of honor rather than a process of shame and fear.

Rustin helped in many other ways. He was immediately put to work writing a leaflet for distribution at the next MIA meeting. In numerous discussions with King, he broadened King's vision by sharing his knowledge and background in the theory and practice of nonviolence. He wrote drafts for many of King's speeches as well as for the first article ever published under King's name, a piece about the boycott entitled "Our Struggle" that appeared in the April issue of *Liberation* magazine.

Seeing in the Montgomery bus boycott the potential for a larger movement, Rustin helped the local leaders understand that they must behave as if appealing to a wide, national, and especially Northern audience. He suggested ideas for keeping the issue of the boycott in the national eye, and he knew who to call for immediate help with transportation for the boycotters.

Years later, in 1986, he recalled that King was about to give up, saying, "I can't go on, these people can't walk anymore. Where are we going to get cars?" Rustin called Randolph in New York and explained the need for cars. Randolph told Rustin to go to Birmingham: "The steel workers there have been making enough money, many of them, to have two cars. Ask them for their second, beat-up car."[5] In recounting the story in 1986, Rustin explained that the black steel workers had been in a position to help because of A. Philip Randolph's threatened March on Washington in 1941. Randolph had called off the march because he had secured the promise that the Fair Employment Practices Commission would be established. As a result of the FEP, blacks in Birmingham had been able to get jobs in the unionized steel industry, which enabled them to buy two cars, which enabled them to donate one to the Montgomery bus boycott in 1956.

Rustin did go to Birmingham and in fact worked mostly out of Birmingham as he assisted with the boycott.

Probably the most important contribution Rustin made to the boycott was to school its leaders, including Martin Luther King Jr., in the tactics of nonviolent protest.

When Rustin arrived, many of the boycott leaders were carrying guns. The homes of King and others were being guarded with rifles and pistols. King was comforted by that protection since he was away a lot, making speeches to raise money for the boycott, and feared for the safety of his wife, Coretta, and their infant daughter, Yolanda. Rustin pointed out that the boycott could not be a truly nonviolent protest with all the guns around.

According to Rustin, King had read about the Gandhi movement in India, but he'd had no direct experience with nonviolence as a protest tactic. Rustin spent many long hours in conversation with King about the philosophy and tactics of nonviolence, often recalling what he had seen and learned in India. As King came to understand the tactic of nonviolence better, he also came to understand how it could be used to make the boycott a success.

Bayard Rustin was pleased to have been of service to King in this way, but he never wished to belittle King's later importance as a spokesman for nonviolence. "I do not believe that one does honor to Dr. King by assuming that, somehow, he had been prepared for this job," Rustin said in 1985. "He had not been prepared for it: either tactically, strategically, or [in] his understanding of nonviolence. The glorious thing is that he came to a profoundly deep understanding of nonviolence through the struggle itself, and through reading and discussion that he had in the process of carrying out the protest, and not that in some way college professors who had read Gandhi had prepared him in advance."[6]

King did indeed grow as a result of the bus boycott. His boyish looks, his eloquence as a speaker, and his deep moral convictions made him a powerful and effective leader. After he and other MIA leaders were indicted, contributions poured into the MIA. The money enabled the organization to purchase vans for local churches to ferry black Montgomeryites back and forth to work. When white insurance agencies refused to write policies on the vans, the MIA got Lloyd's of London to give them insurance. As the boycott continued, many whites in Montgomery tried using violence and intimidation to end the boycott. The boycotters, with few exceptions, refused to back down, and did not fight back. Many people across the nation began to recognize that a great moral force was at work. As the most visible boycott leader, Martin Luther King Jr. was closely identified with that moral force.

The blacks of Montgomery stayed off the city buses for over a year. Though the months wore on, their determination rarely flagged. White women who had earlier threatened to fire their black maids and baby-sitters if they observed the boycott eventually realized they needed the household help and drove their employees to and from work.

The city of Montgomery lost a great deal of money by keeping the buses running nearly empty, because the vast majority of its riders had always been black; most whites owned cars. In addition, white businessmen in Montgomery lost money because their black patrons found it difficult to travel to the downtown shopping center. These white businessmen began to put pressure on the city and bus company to give in to the boycotters' demands.

Meanwhile, the nine justices of the United States Supreme Court finally heard the Rosa Parks case, and on November 13, 1956, they ruled that segregation on the Montgomery buses was unconstitutional. King asked Montgomery's blacks to continue the boycott until the written order arrived from the highest court in the land. The written order was delivered to city officials on December 20, 1956, and the following day, the boycotters returned to the buses. King, E. D. Nixon, and other leaders of the MIA personally rode the first integrated bus in Montgomery.

Integration did not go smoothly at first. White snipers fired at buses; the homes of King and others were bombed. Rosa Parks and her family received telephone death threats; not long afterward they moved to Detroit, Michigan. Eventually, however, the furor died down, and bus integration was grudgingly accepted in Montgomery.

Bayard Rustin was proud of his role in the success of the Montgomery bus boycott and prouder still that his grandmother was alive to see it. Julia Davis Rustin died in 1957, the same year as the newly formed civil rights organization, the Southern Christian Leadership Conference, undertook its first major demonstration— the Prayer Pilgrimage for Freedom in Washington, D.C.—which Bayard organized.

CHAPTER SIX

THE SOUTHERN CHRISTIAN LEADERSHIP CONFERENCE

As the case of the Montgomery bus boycott was wending its way through the courts, other civil rights efforts were going on as well. The NAACP was continuing its campaign for school integration by challenging admissions practices at the all-white University of Alabama. After a three-and-a-half-year court fight, masterminded and argued before the United States Supreme Court by NAACP attorney Thurgood Marshall, a twenty-six-year-old black woman named Autherine Lucy won the right to register at the university in the fall of 1956. Her registration caused a series of violent outbursts in the white community, and she stayed only a few weeks. She withdrew and sued the university for barring her from the school dormitories.

A. Philip Randolph decided to hold a meeting in support of Autherine Lucy at Madison Square Garden in New York. He asked Rustin and William Sutherland (the same man who had, with Rustin, defied Randolph back in 1947) to organize it.

They invited Eleanor Roosevelt, widow of the late president Franklin D. Roosevelt, to speak. They knew that Adam Clayton Powell Jr. had to be invited to speak as well.

Congressman Adam Clayton Powell Jr. considered New York

Bayard's grandmother Julia Davis Rustin, who raised him, was a major influence in his life. *Courtesy of the Bayard Rustin Fund.*

Bayard was a running guard on his West Chester, Pennsylvania, high school's championship football team (1931–32). *Courtesy of the Bayard Rustin Fund.*

During World War II, the Quaker-raised Rustin took the unpopular position of objecting to America's entrance into the conflict. But he also worked hard to secure rights for African Americans serving in the military. *Courtesy of the Bayard Rustin Fund.*

Bayard Rustin was one of many who participated in the 1947 Journey of Reconciliation. From left to right: Worth Randle, Wallace Nelson, Ernest Bromley, James Peck, Igal Roodenko, Bayard Rustin, Joseph Felmet, George Houser, and Andrew Johnson. *Courtesty of the Bayard Rustin Fund.*

Mahatma Ghandi (left), leader of the Indian Independence movement, led a march to the sea at Dandi, India, to collect salt, in violation of the British law. On the right is a lieutenant, Mrs. Sarojini Naidu. *Courtesy of UPI/Corbis-Bettman.*

Rustin was an active participant in various African independence movements. Here he is pictured in 1952 with Nnamdi Azikiwe; one year later, Azikiwe was elected premier of East Nigeria. *Courtesy of the Bayard Rustin Fund.*

Rustin worked with the Reverend Martin Luther King Jr. on many occasions in the 1950s and 1960s (1962). *Courtesy of the Bayard Rustin Fund.*

Adam Clayton Powell Jr., a New York congressman from Harlem, was an influential and charismatic figure on the civil rights scene (1955). *Courtesy of UPI/Bettman.*

In the early 1960s, Rustin had several debates with Malcolm X, a chief spokesman for the Nation of Islam. From left to right: Bayard Rustin, Malcolm X, Michael Winston (1961). *Courtesy of Spingarn Research Center, Howard University Archives.*

Several days before the 1963 March on Washington, Bayard Rustin pauses to speak from his office balcony. *Courtesy of Sam Falk/New York Times Pictures.*

After the hugely successful march, the two major organizers, Bayard Rustin (right) and his friend and mentor, A. Philip Randolph, pose in front of the Lincoln Memorial. *Courtesy of Leonard McCombe, Life magazine, Time, Inc.*

This photo, taken at the 1963 March on Washington from the top of the Lincoln Memorial, shows the crowd—an estimated one quarter million—on either side of the reflecting pool. *Courtesy of UPI/Bettman.*

In his later years, Bayard Rustin became very involved with the International Rescue Committee, working on behalf of refugee groups around the world. Here he is with a group of El Salvadoran children (1983). *Courtesy of the Bayard Rustin Fund.*

Courtesy of the Bayard Rustin Fund.

City his territory. The outspoken black minister of Abyssinian Baptist Church in Harlem had led protests for jobs for African Americans back in the 1930s and had won election to Congress from Harlem every two years since 1945. Any big civil rights–related event in New York City had better involve Powell. Rustin recalled that the planned agenda had Mrs. Roosevelt speaking last. "She had to come late, and furthermore, Mrs. Roosevelt, being so popular among blacks, would be the best last speaker, because if Adam got going toward the end, God knows when he would stop."[1]

On the evening of the event, the program was well along and Adam Clayton Powell was nowhere to be found. Rustin remembered: "Adam didn't come and didn't come, and Mr. Randolph was putting on all sorts of minor people to fill in the time, and he says to me, 'You've gotta find Adam.' All of a sudden, the place goes black. You can't see a thing. Mr. Randolph is calling over to me, 'Bayard, Bayard, what is happening?' I'm stumbling around backstage, trying to find somebody to look at the lights, whereupon a great spotlight hits the back of the auditorium, and there stands Adam. He comes down the line waving to the people.

"Somebody says, 'Hey, Adam!' And he's yelling and screaming and walking, and [the audience is] just getting built up and built up and built up. The minute he hits the stage, Mr. Randolph attempts to stand up to introduce him, and the crowd is now going, 'We want Adam! We want Adam!' Mr. Randolph can't even introduce him . . .

"And then Adam is speaking and speaking and speaking, and we have to be out of the place by eleven o'clock, and I make a great mistake. I wrote a note, which I always did for Mr. Randolph on these occasions: 'Dear Adam, Mr. Randolph asked me to ask you to cut your speech short. For every five minutes we are here after eleven o'clock, it costs us a thousand dollars, money we do not have. Mrs. Roosevelt has not spoken yet, and she has been promised to speak last. Will you please hurry up?'

"So I go up and lay this on the podium, whereupon Adam looks at me as if I'm dirt and sweeps me away, for which the crowd claps. He then picks up the thing. He says, 'I've got a note here from somebody. Bay-ard Rust-in. Anybody ever hear of him?' The crowd says, 'No! Who's he?' He says, 'He tells me that if we're not out of here by eleven o'clock, it's going to cost us a thousand dollars—every minute.' He says, 'Can I ask you a question?' 'Yes!' goes the crowd. 'Do you have to pay for freedom?' The crowd roars, 'Yes!' 'Do we believe in paying for freedom?' 'Yes!' the crowd roars back. 'Does anybody think we should stop having this important meeting because it's going to cost us something?' The crowd roars, 'No, Adam!'

"He says, 'I will tell this what's-his-name, Bay-ard Rust-in.' He throws the paper away. 'I will stand here and we will stand here all night if necessary to tell the world, to tell the government, to tell the president of the United States, we want freedom and we are willing to pay for it.' And the crowd just goes wild. He waits and quiets them at their height. And he says, 'I want to tell you when the bill comes, this Bay-ard Rust-in can send the bill to Abyssinian Baptist Church, and we'll pay for the freedom we are having tonight.' The place goes crazy.

"We had a five-thousand-dollar bill to pay as a result of this. You know, you have to pay the extra for the ushers' overtime, the security men's overtime. To this day, neither Randolph nor I ever got a penny of that money from Adam Powell. I had to go to Roy Wilkins [of the NAACP] to get that money to pay that bill."[2]

To be sure, there were some very large egos among the civil rights leaders. Experiences such as the one with Adam Clayton Powell taught Bayard Rustin important lessons about the necessity of dealing with large egos—lessons that would come in handy when he organized the March on Washington.

The success of the Montgomery bus boycott presented a major opportunity for civil rights leaders and organizations to build on the movement that had begun in Montgomery. Soon after the victory of the boycott, blacks in other cities began mounting their own challenges to bus segregation. The leaders of the major civil rights organizations each wanted their organizations to spearhead the shaping of the scattered protests occurring throughout the South into a coherent civil rights movement. While their desire to do so stemmed largely from their conviction that their organizations were best equipped to do so, ego also played a role.

Now there was a new leader who had tasted civil rights victory and wanted more. Martin Luther King Jr. felt a tremendous letdown after the Montgomery bus boycott ended. His question was, where do we go from here? Bayard Rustin urged King to form a Southern-based civil rights organization. At King's request, he drew up a plan for an organization he called the Southern Leadership Conference.

The plan called for a group of primarily Southern black ministers to take charge of a drive for civil rights in their region. King approved, but insisted on calling the organization the Southern *Christian* Leadership Conference (SCLC). Rustin advised against the new name, pointing out that it could alienate Jews, who were strong supporters of the fledgling civil rights movement, and blacks who had turned away from Christianity and joined the Nation of Islam (commonly known as Black Muslims). King would not be talked out of his decision, though, and he proved to be right; the name did not alienate non-Christians who supported its cause.

The SCLC decided to concentrate on Southern black voting rights, believing that the right to vote was the key to gaining other rights. With the vote, blacks, who were in the majority in some areas of the South, would have a say in who their elected officials were. Having to be responsible to their voters, these officials would pass laws eliminating segregation. The SCLC decided to stage a Prayer Pilgrimage for Freedom in Washington, D.C., to mobilize the support of the Christian ministry across the country.

The SCLC also sought the support of A. Philip Randolph, Roy Wilkins of the NAACP, and other organizations. Wilkins had joined the NAACP in 1931 at the age of thirty as assistant to Walter White, who was then executive director. As head of the oldest black civil rights organization—the NAACP was founded in 1909 on the one-hundredth anniversary of the birth of Abraham Lincoln—Wilkins adhered to the longtime philosophy of the NAACP, which was to make friends, not enemies, among politicians, and to pursue through legal means, primarily the courts, equal rights for blacks. His organization had a sizable budget and many important white supporters; it had accomplished a great deal, although progress had been slow. Wilkins was at first reluctant to have anything to do with the SCLC, fearing that the new organization would threaten the NAACP's activities in the South. Also Wilkins preferred to work through the courts and disapproved of mass actions such as the bus boycott. Still he agreed to take part in a planning session in Washington, D.C., that was attended by more than seventy representatives from various civil rights, labor, pacifist, and religious organizations. The group chose the date May 17, 1957, because it was the third anniversary of the Supreme Court decision in *Brown v. Board of Education, Topeka*.

Wilkins stood with Randolph and King to announce the plans to the press and to state the five objectives of the Prayer Pilgrimage for Freedom: to demonstrate black unity, to provide an opportunity for Northerners to show their support, to protest ongoing legal attacks on the NAACP by Southern states, to protest violence in the South, and to urge the passage of civil rights legislation. At the press conference, King voiced his hope that Congress would pass a civil rights bill giving the Justice Department power to file lawsuits against discriminatory registration and voting practices in the South.

A. Philip Randolph selected Bayard Rustin to organize the Prayer Pilgrimage. Rustin was then executive director of the War Resisters League, a pacifist organization, but he took an official leave to help Randolph. Drawing from his experiences organizing the 1941 March on Washington that never took place, Rustin worked with other organizers to plan the day's events and to publicize the Pilgrimage to ensure a large turnout. He also submitted drafts for the first national address by Dr. King. Rustin urged King to emphasize the importance of nonviolence in the civil rights struggle. Both he and an associate, Stanley Levison—a white lawyer from New York with whom he had formed a group called In Friendship the previous year to raise money for Southern civil rights causes—suggested that King also emphasize the importance of cooperation between Southern black leaders and white union members in bringing about integration.

The turnout for the Pilgrimage was lighter than its organizers had hoped. They had planned for fifty thousand people; some twenty thousand showed up at noon at the Lincoln Memorial. But they gave enthusiastic applause to King's speech, which was entitled "Give Us the Ballot." King had listened to Rustin's and Levison's counsel, but had chosen to emphasize voting rights.

In Rustin's view, the 1957 Prayer Pilgrimage was a turning point, both for Martin Luther King Jr. and for the Southern-based nonviolent civil rights movement. It brought King north, and introduced him to the Northern labor movement, which then began to contribute money to the SCLC. Moreover, the Prayer Pilgrimage was the first of several marches that year at which King played a central role and was projected onto the national stage.

Following the Prayer Pilgrimage, Rustin continued to work as an unofficial, New York–based aide to King, all the while remaining on the payroll of the War Resisters League. With King and Levison, he organized a meeting of the SCLC in Montgomery in early August. At that meeting King announced a Crusade for Citizenship to encourage blacks to seek the vote. Rustin was hired to coordinate the rallies that would kick off the crusade the following February.

On August 29, 1957, Congress passed the first Civil Rights Act since the post–Civil War Reconstruction period. But it fell far short of what civil rights activists had hoped for. While it established a civil rights commission and allowed the Justice Department to file voting rights suits against discriminatory Southern registrars, there were few provisions to guarantee compliance. Without specific reprisals for noncompliance, such as the cut-off of federal funds or federal takeover of voter registration, the act was little more than words on paper.

Rustin continued his organizing for the Crusade for Citizenship, working behind the scenes from New York. It was too risky for him to travel to the South, for it might expose King to charges of associating with a "Communist-conscientious-objector-homosexual." King reluctantly agreed to this arrangement, although he had come to depend a great deal on Rustin's counsel. Ella Baker, who had been serving as executive secretary of In Friendship, the fund-raising organization, went to the South in Rustin's place.

The campaign was a great disappointment. One major problem was that the NAACP announced its own crusade to register black voters in the South; the older organization eclipsed the SCLC's efforts. Soon the SCLC decided to drop its emphasis on voting rights and turn to the campaign for school desegregation.

Although the United States Supreme Court had ruled school segregation unconstitutional in 1954, it had not set a deadline for integration. Rather, the court had ordered that integration should proceed "with all deliberate speed." For white segregationists, that meant the next century at the earliest, certainly not in their lifetimes. Local school boards resisted integration at every turn. The first major crisis occurred in Little Rock, Arkansas, in September 1957, where none other than the governor of the state, Orville Faubus, barred the door to Little Rock's Central High School to prevent nine black students from entering. Republican President Dwight D. Eisenhower, who had signed the Civil Rights Act a month earlier, reluctantly ordered federal troops to Little Rock to prevent further interference with integration.

A. Philip Randolph and Bayard Rustin realized that the events in Little Rock could be the basis of a national civil rights movement. Unlike the Montgomery bus boycott, a local protest, and the Prayer Pilgrimage, a religious event, the issue of school integration in Little Rock was of national importance. They decided to stage a Youth March for Integrated Schools in Washington, D.C. With the support of a coalition of civil rights organizations and Martin Luther King as honorary chairman, Bayard Rustin organized the march. Originally scheduled for October 11, it had to be postponed after King, in New York signing copies of his new book about the Montgomery bus boycott, *Stride Toward Freedom*, was stabbed by a deranged black woman. The march was held on October 25, and Coretta King stood in for her husband. Some ten thousand students joined the march down Constitution Avenue to the Lincoln Memorial.

Believing that King's absence had accounted for the comparatively low turnout, Randolph made plans for a second Youth March for Integrated Schools in Washington, D.C., on April 18, 1959. Once again, Bayard Rustin was the chief organizer, and this time Roy Wilkins agreed to support the march. Attendance was more than double that of the first. Following the march, a delegation of student representatives approached the White House and sought a meeting with the president. A presidential assistant was dispatched to meet with them instead. Bayard Rustin believed that the students' disappointment in not seeing the president helped lay the groundwork for the next, more confrontational, stage of the civil rights movement:

"When Ike refused to receive those youngsters, two of those who went back to organize SNCC [Student Nonviolent Coordinating Committee, pronounced "snick"] in North Carolina were two of the youngsters who were denied the right to enter the White House, who lost faith that it was possible to do anything with Ike . . . Vote with your feet, you cannot do anything at the White House. So that there was a definite connection between the two Marches for Integrated Schools and the creation of SNCC."[3]

Less than two years later, on February 1, 1960, a group of students from the all-black North Carolina Agricultural & Technical College in Greensboro sat in at a local Woolworth's lunch counter and refused to leave until they were served. They were arrested and taken to jail, and their places were taken by other black students. Soon white students had joined the cause, and the sit-in movement spread like wildfire throughout the South. A new era had begun in which Southern blacks and their supporters deliberately broke segregation laws and exposed themselves to arrest and bodily injury in order to fight for equal rights.

Twenty years earlier, Rustin, Farmer, and other members of CORE had sat in at restaurants in Chicago to protest segregation; their movement had not spread. It was a case of the confluence of events. The students in 1960 had the inspiration of the successful Montgomery bus boycott to draw upon, as well as the beginnings of a new attitude on the part of the federal government about the meaning of equal rights.

Ella Baker, one of the founders of In Friendship who was then working with the SCLC, was excited by the students' spontaneous efforts and believed that if they were well organized, they could be a powerful force in the civil rights movement. She contacted some of the students and arranged a meeting at Shaw University in Raleigh, North Carolina. Some two hundred students attended the meeting, and King was there to lend his support and give an address. Out of that meeting came SNCC, which Rustin hoped to help in any way he could. Unfortunately other events intruded to separate him from both SNCC and the SCLC.

That year, 1960, was an election year. A. Philip Randolph was making plans for a March on the Republican and Democratic nominating conventions in July. He had staged such marches every four years since 1948, and Bayard Rustin had helped organize nearly all of them. The fact that in May 1960 Congress had passed another Civil Rights Act made no difference to Randolph and Rustin. Again, it was a weak act that did not meet the needs of Southern black people. In early June, Martin Luther King Jr. traveled to New York with

Randolph to jointly announce the March on Conventions Movement for Freedom Now.

But Adam Clayton Powell Jr. did not want Randolph's and King's forces to march. By 1960, the congressman from New York's Harlem had become the most senior member of the House Committee on Education and Labor. By rights he should replace retiring chairman Graham Barden at the end of the 1959 session. But Powell had powerful enemies in Congress, and a move was afoot to deny him the chairmanship. He wanted to avoid any situation that would reflect badly on him. That may have been why he did not want the marches at the conventions.

Another possible reason, however, was Powell's huge ego. Flamboyant in his personal style, he loved to make whites uncomfortable. He believed that most blacks, rather than being jealous of his numerous houses, cars, and expensive suits, looked to him as a role model, someone who could "tell Whitey where to get off." Powell was so accustomed to being the most powerful black man in America that he resented the rise to prominence of Martin Luther King Jr. He especially did not like the idea that Randolph and King were joining forces. He had nothing against Randolph, who had supported him in many causes in the past, but he had no compunction about hurting a close associate of Randolph's if it suited his purposes. He began a campaign to drive a wedge between the two men, using Bayard Rustin as the wedge. In a speech at a church conference in Buffalo, he denounced the two men as being "captives of behind-the-scenes forces." He charged that King was controlled by Rustin and that Randolph was controlled by "socalist interests."[4] When the two men did not dignify Powell's remarks with public responses, Powell threatened King that he would tell the press that King and Rustin had a homosexual relationship.

While the charge was untrue, King feared the damage it would cause. Rustin felt strongly that King should not back down in the face of Powell's threats, but he knew King was agonizing over what to do. So Rustin decided to take matters into his own hands. He resigned as special assistant to King and director of the SCLC's New York office. He fully expected King to refuse to accept his resignation. To his great disappointment, King did accept it.

Surprisingly, any anger Rustin felt at the time did not last. He was not even bitter at Powell. As he explained in 1986, "I think this was a pretty miserable thing for Adam to do, but like many people in the black community Adam had mesmerized all of us. If somebody else had done this it would have been a horrible thing, but somehow or other you got to the point where you expected these shenanigans from Adam."[5]

The planned marches at the conventions went on without Rustin, with King and Randolph in the lead, in spite of Powell's attempts to halt them. The marches did not, however, draw substantial crowds or attract much press interest.

Another similar blow was to come for Rustin. He was scheduled to speak at a SNCC conference in Atlanta in October. Then officials from one of the local unions sponsoring the conference threatened to cancel a funding grant if Rustin appeared on the program. Reluctantly, the students disinvited Rustin, pleading financial necessity.

The next three years were the most tumultuous of the Southern civil rights movement, but Bayard Rustin had little public role in connection with either King or the movement during that time. He did, however, remain close to SNCC and had several debates with Malcolm X.

Malcolm X was National Minister for the Nation of Islam, commonly called the Black Muslims. Founded in the 1940s by a man named W. D. Fard, who had since died, the Nation was now headed by Elijah Muhammad and headquartered in Chicago. The Black Muslims followed world Islam in their worship of Allah and in their observance of dietary restrictions such as disdaining alcohol and pork. But they departed from world Islam in their hatred of whites, whom they called devils. They also emphasized a form of black nationalism by encouraging the faithful to start their own businesses and become economically independent of whites.

The Black Muslims had attracted many converts, especially among black prisoners. The most famous convict convert was a man born Malcolm Little. Like many Black Muslims, Malcolm had taken an *X* for his last name to symbolize the fact that his real name had been lost in slavery, only to be replaced by a slave name.

On his release from prison, Malcolm X had gone to work for Elijah Muhammad. He had proved to be a charismatic speaker, capable of winning many new converts. Appointed an assistant minister in 1953, he had succeeded in establishing Muslim temples in Boston, Philadelphia, and New York, and was rewarded with appointment as minister of Temple No. 7 in New York City. In the media capital of the world, Malcolm X became famous for his outspoken contempt for whites. The defiant congressman Adam Clayton Powell Jr. was spending much of his time outside the country because of various lawsuits and tax troubles, so Malcolm X took up the reins of militancy.

Bayard Rustin had met Malcolm X and liked him personally. Although he could not accept the philosophy of the Black Muslims, he understood its attraction for many disaffected Northern blacks. He knew that Malcolm X and the Muslims were forces to be reckoned with, and understood that if the mainstream civil rights organizations could not alter their strategy to fit the new order, they would be left in the dust. He had several debates with Malcolm X during the late 1950s and early 1960s, representing the integrationist, mainstream viewpoint against Malcolm X's separatist ideology.

But Rustin's attention was also very focused on the international scene. He spent most of 1961 and 1962 in Tanzania and Northern Rhodesia. Northern Rhodesia was seeking independence from Great Britain, and the leader of the independence movement, Kenneth Kaunda, asked Rustin to work in Tanzania in a movement called the World Peace Brigade. Rustin's job, as usual, was to be an organizer—specifically, to organize a March on Northern Rhodesia to pressure the British Parliament into holding a vote on the question of Northern Rhodesian independence. It was part of a massive civil disobedience campaign to gain independence. Rustin worked for months to get people from all over the world to come, and in June 1962, people from twenty-two countries, including hundreds of thousands of Africans, marched up to the border of Northern Rhodesia. The British quickly agreed to put the question of independence to the vote. That same year, the blacks of Northern Rhodesia were given a much larger say in the affairs of the country, which remained a British protectorate until 1964. At that point, the newly independent nation took the name Zambia, and Kenneth Kaunda was its first president.

CHAPTER SEVEN

TO MARCH OR NOT TO MARCH

By the time Bayard Rustin returned to the United States in late 1962, the nature of the civil rights struggle had undergone a fundamental change. Beginning with the student sit-in movement that led to the founding of SNCC, a new era of confrontation was ushered in.

The seeds planted by the student sit-in movement were nurtured by a dramatic tactic on the part of CORE in 1961—the Freedom Rides. Just as the 1947 Journey of Reconciliation had been undertaken to test the 1946 U.S. Supreme Court decision against segregation on interstate transportation, the Freedom Rides were a test of a similar ruling by the highest court. In a decision handed down in December 1960 in the case of *Boynton v. Virginia*, the court held that segregation in waiting rooms and restaurants serving interstate bus passengers was unconstitutional. At the time, CORE was still a small organization; it had never grown the way its founders had hoped, twenty years earlier. James Farmer, one of the original founders, had just been named CORE's national director. Bayard Rustin was no longer formally associated with the organization.

CORE's idea was to send an interracial group of people, all trained in nonviolence, on a bus ride through the South, testing bus facilities. There was no question that they would encounter violent resistance, for they would travel through the staunchly racist Deep South, and the resulting publicity would give CORE a national platform.

The Freedom Rides began on May 4, 1961. White segregationists were already angry and upset over the civil rights movement and determined not to give blacks and their white friends another inch in the fight over segregation. In several cities, Freedom Riders were severely beaten. The injured included John Lewis, the youngest of the group, a member of SNCC and a student at seminary school in Nashville, Tennessee; and James Peck, who had been on the 1947 Journey of Reconciliation fourteen years before, and since then had served as editor of one of CORE's publications. A Freedom Ride bus was burned in Anniston, Alabama. Throughout the Freedom Rides, the riders were harassed and threatened and intimidated. Yet they refused to give up and sang freedom songs to keep up their courage.

When members of the first group were arrested or so brutally beaten that they could not go on, a contingent of students from Nashville stepped in to continue the original Freedom Ride. When they too were arrested, students, ministers, and others came in waves from across the country, filling the prisons in states like Alabama.

The Freedom Rides were a brief moment in the civil rights movement, but they captured the attention of the nation in a way that few other campaigns in the struggle had. They especially inspired Southern blacks—for them, the term *Freedom Rider* came to mean civil rights worker.

That was the most important legacy of the Freedom Rides. It is certainly true that they were crucial as a "shocking challenge to the old order," as absolute proof that thousands of people were willing to put their lives on the line and face pain and even death for what they believed in. But even more important, the Freedom Rides were deci-sive in pulling together the previously scattered attacks on segrega-tion into a true *movement*.

The South became more resistant, and response to civil rights demonstrations became ever more violent. In the fall of 1962, a young man named James Meredith attempted to enroll at the University of Mississippi. Governor Ross Barnett urged whites to "stand up like men and tell them 'Never.'" Only after President John F. Kennedy sent in federal troops and a riot injured hundreds and killed two was Meredith finally registered.

The confrontational tactics of SNCC and CORE had taken precedence over the more passive boycotts and marches. To maintain leadership in the movement, King and the SCLC were forced to adopt similar tactics. In the spring of 1963, the SCLC conducted a huge desegregation campaign in Birmingham, Alabama. The concept of nonviolence was sorely tested as scores of demonstrators were beaten, poked with cattle prods, and set upon with fire hoses and police dogs. Hundreds were jailed—including King himself—in Birmingham.

Bayard Rustin and A. Philip Randolph despaired of what was going on, and they worried about what lay ahead. They believed that the federal government would soon pass strong civil rights laws guaranteeing equal voting rights and an end to segregation in the South. But what of the North? All the unrest and violence in the South was bound to spill over into the North, for while changes were occurring in the Southern states, no similar changes were taking place in the top half of the country.

In the North, the problem for blacks was not legal segregation but de facto segregation—segregation in fact. It would eventually become a problem for blacks in the South as well. The main factor was an economic one. It mattered little that blacks were permitted to eat in white restaurants if they could not afford to pay for their meals. Unless blacks could get jobs to improve their lives, they could never really exercise their new legal freedoms.

A. Philip Randolph believed that the mainstream civil rights organizations had become too competitive in attracting media exposure and contributions. He believed they should cooperate on a major initiative to show the nation, and themselves, that they could work together. Randolph had long dreamed of a mass March on Washington. Bayard Rustin and two young colleagues, Norman Hill and Tom Kahn, persuaded him that now was the time for it. The mass demonstration would be called the March on Washington for Jobs and Freedom, and—unlike the aborted black marches planned in the 1940s—it would be an integrated march.

Randolph contacted the leaders of all the major civil rights organizations. He was disappointed that neither Roy Wilkins of the NAACP nor Whitney Young of the National Urban League was interested. The same was true of Walter Reuther, head of the United Auto Workers (UAW), one of the most powerful (mostly white) labor unions. All three leaders believed that it was the wrong time to march, and that any such massive protest in the nation's capital would damage the close relationships they and their organizations had managed to cultivate with federal officials and members of Congress. They believed that the violent response by white segregationists to the Freedom Rides and to the Birmingham campaign had awakened most people in the government, from President Kennedy on down, to the need for strong civil rights legislation. Staging a March on Washington at this point would only anger these men.

They were right. President Kennedy had learned of the proposed march and was making every effort to prevent it. He called on important friends of the civil rights and labor movements and asked them to do what they could to keep the march from going forward. He also went on national television on June 11, 1963, to respond directly to the violence in Birmingham, saying: "We are confronted primarily with a moral issue. It is as old as the Scriptures and as clear as the American Constitution. The heart of the question is whether all Americans are afforded equal rights and equal opportunities; whether we are going to treat our fellow Americans as we want to be treated. If an American because his skin is dark cannot eat lunch in a restaurant open to the public, if he cannot send his children to the best public school available, if he cannot vote for the public officials who represent him, if in short he cannot enjoy the full and free life which all of us want, then who among us would be content to have the color of his skin changed and stand in his place? Who among us would then be content with the counsels of patience and delay?"[1]

The following evening, as if in response to the president's message, a segregationist named Byron DeLaBeckwith assassinated Medgar Evers, an NAACP field secretary in Jackson, Mississippi.

But Martin Luther King Jr. had a strong feeling that both the president's speech and the assassination of Evers indicated the time was right for A. Philip Randolph's March on Washington. Once King was on board, Randolph believed he would get the other civil rights and labor leaders behind the march.

President Kennedy then introduced the strongest civil rights bill yet to Congress. Unlike the bills of 1957 and 1960, it contained provisions for real enforcement. Still, if the president had hoped his announcement of the bill would lead to the cancellation of the march, he was wrong. The day after Kennedy introduced the bill,

King spoke publicly about the march, and the following day, Randolph instructed that the march be officially announced. He believed that the march would put pressure on Congress to pass Kennedy's proposed civil rights bill. A peaceful demonstration in the nation's capital would show the strength of the civil rights movement, and show it in the most positive way.

President Kennedy personally called the major civil rights and labor leaders to the White House to ask that the march not go forward. Afterward the leaders met privately. While no one wanted to alienate the president, everyone believed in Randolph's march.

But critics of the march continued to work against it. Many political and business leaders argued that the atmosphere in the country had become too violent, and that a large group of people descending on Washington would most certainly attract violent opposition. If the march were marred by violence—on the part of either marchers or their enemies—the civil rights cause would be seriously hurt.

Some segregationists even went so far as to label the march a communist plot. Two Southern governors, Ross Barnett of Mississippi and George Wallace of Alabama, called a press conference and charged that Martin Luther King Jr. was a communist. As proof, they displayed a huge photograph of King making a 1957 speech at Highlander Folk School in Tennessee. The school had been established to help workers learn how to fight for their rights. Barnett and Wallace called the school a "communist training school." Barnett went even further, asserting that the president and his brother, Attorney General Robert Kennedy, were "assisting a red racial plot."[2]

President Kennedy was furious over these charges. Although the longtime FBI director, J. Edgar Hoover, had insisted that King was a communist, neither the president nor his brother believed it. King did have some close supporters, however, who had also supported communist causes. In this, King and the SCLC were no different than other major civil rights organizations and leaders. But the issue of King and communism threatened to derail the march. President Kennedy asked King to disassociate himself from two key supporters with known communist ties, Stanley Levison and Jack O'Dell. Reluctantly, King did so. After that, Kennedy made no further attempts to halt the march. In fact, on July 17 he called a press conference to state that recent government investigations had shown that none of the civil rights leaders was a communist and none of the civil rights demonstrations was communist inspired. He further stated that he looked forward to being in Washington on the day of the march and urged any citizen who wished to do so to exercise his or her right to march.

Meanwhile, the six major civil rights leaders had met on July 2 to begin planning the march. Attending the meeting were A. Philip Randolph, Roy Wilkins of the NAACP, Whitney M. Young Jr. of the National Urban League, James Farmer of CORE, Martin Luther King Jr. of the SCLC, and John Lewis of SNCC. Nine others had expected to attend the meeting, including Bayard Rustin as Randolph's deputy. But Wilkins insisted that only the leaders meet.

One of the major topics of discussion was who would organize the march. Randolph said he had dreamed of a March on Washington for twenty years and that he wanted Rustin to be the chief organizer. Wilkins and Young were adamantly against Rustin's holding any public position. His past communist ties, his socialism, his conscientious-objector status during World War II, and his known homosexuality would be used against the march. While King and Farmer knew firsthand of Rustin's organizational skills, they agreed with Wilkins and Young. John Lewis did not express an opinion. But Randolph was adamant. Why didn't Randolph himself lead the march? the others asked. Randolph replied that he would, but in that case insisted on the right to appoint Rustin as his deputy. The others bowed to Randolph out of respect. The march, after all, was his idea. But they warned him to expect trouble.

The trouble came as anticipated. Two weeks before the march, Senator Strom Thurmond of South Carolina rose on the floor of the Senate and attacked Rustin as a draft dodger, a homosexual, and a communist. Any march that Rustin organized had to be anti-American, said Thurmond.

The controversy over Rustin could have derailed the march, but Randolph knew how to deal with Thurmond's denunciation of his aide. After consulting with other march leaders, he called a press conference. There, with the other leaders beside him, he issued a single short statement: "We, the leaders of the March on Washington, have absolute confidence in Bayard Rustin's character and abilities."[3] He then refused to answer any questions about Rustin.

Reporters tried to get the other leaders to talk about Rustin. But the other five presented a united front. The only answer they would give was "As Mr. Randolph has said . . ." After a while, the reporters stopped asking.

In return for their support of Randolph on the Rustin issue, Wilkins and Young insisted that the Leadership Conference on Civil Rights be part of the planning. Randolph had envisioned the march leadership being entirely black, but he agreed to allow four white labor and religious leaders in on the planning of the march.

Randolph chose the date: Wednesday, August 28. It had no particular historical significance. Randolph wanted a summer march, to give militant black youth something positive to do. The ten march leaders agreed that it would take place on the Mall and that it would begin at the Washington Monument and end one mile away at the Lincoln Memorial. The tone of the march would be positive—a massive peaceful display of black and white citizens urging justice and equal rights now.

CHAPTER EIGHT

MARCH ORGANIZER

With less than two months to plan the largest peaceful march in American history, Bayard Rustin had his work cut out for him. He had to publicize the march to attract hundreds of thousands of people. He had to make arrangements to provide parking for buses and private cars in which those people would travel, and provide food and drink and sanitary facilities for them as well. He had to arrange for first aid for those who were overcome by the heat that typified late August in Washington, D.C. He had to make sure that the hundreds of thousands of participants remained peaceful throughout the day, and have a security system in place, ready to act, if there were threats to that peace.

He also had to contend with big egos: those of the ten civil rights, labor, and religious leaders who wanted a say in the arrangements, and all of whom wanted to be part of the main speakers program; and those of the president and members of Congress, who wanted the march to reflect well on them, and knew that a poorly attended march or a march that degenerated into violence would harm their chances of reelection. He also had to satisfy the marchers, who would be traveling far and standing as well as marching in the hot sun and would want to hear inspiring speeches, emotion-laden songs, and to feel that all they'd been through was worth it.

It was a tall order, even for Bayard Rustin, who had spent the better part of his life organizing one thing or another—groups, protests, marches. He had organized the massive march on the borders of Northern Rhodesia a little more than a year earlier. He had organized the Aldermaston peace march in England, a demonstration in the Sahara Desert protesting France's atom-bomb test there, and a march against anti-Semitism in Germany. He had organized the 1941 March on Washington that had never happened. He had organized the Journey of Reconciliation in 1947, and the Prayer Pilgrimage and Youth Marches in 1957. But he had never, ever organized a march like the August 28, 1963, March on Washington.

Two days after Randolph named him deputy director of the march, Rustin prepared a memo for his mentor outlining his plan. All ten cochairmen would have representatives at march headquarters and all decisions would be made cooperatively. It would have been much easier for him to have made these decisions alone, but he understood that the march was important to all the leaders. Rustin had made it understood that he did not expect to act alone; then he proceeded to make most of the major decisions—with the agreement of the representatives of the cochairmen.

There were so many things needed to make the march a success. One big need was money. If the march was to bring thousands of people, many of them poor and unemployed, to Washington, D.C., then there had to be money to finance their trips. Rustin figured out how much money would be needed to transport and house the people.

An equally big need was promotion. There was no point in providing for one hundred thousand individuals at the march if very few people knew that it was to take place. The march committee had to spend money for printing and distributing press releases and flyers to attract marchers. They had to print up detailed instructions for the marchers, telling them where to go, what to do, and where to find food and drink. The committee had to print up signs for the marchers to carry. Bayard Rustin estimated that for printing materials alone, ten thousand dollars would be needed. Rustin and other members of the march committee worked tirelessly to raise money. Both the NAACP and the National Urban League made substantial contributions, and so did the trade unions. Fortunately, as word of the march got out, individual people also sent contributions. Especially appreciated were the small gifts sent by people who would like to have attended the march but were too old or had too many responsibilities to do so. While these contributions were small—one to ten dollars usually—they told Bayard Rustin that there was a groundswell of public support for the march.

Meanwhile, organizations and individuals held their own fundraisers, from bake sales to car washes, from fashion shows to house parties.

Bayard Rustin understood that people determined to participate would get to Washington, D.C., by hook or by crook. One of his many challenges was to discourage private cars and encourage bus and train travel—for obvious reasons, considering the number of parking spaces available in Washington, D.C. The NAACP, the National Urban League, and various labor unions that had agreed to participate in the march pledged to provide buses, some free of charge, others for a small fee.

But that gave rise to another problem: where to park the buses. Rustin persuaded District officials to ban parking in a large section of Northwest Washington. He then proceeded with plans to provide each bus with a captain who would have an envelope of instructions: where to park the bus, when it was supposed to leave the capital, and where passengers could go for help in locating their buses.

For marchers arriving by train, Rustin worked out a plan with the railroads and the District's Union Station under which dozens of special trains would be provided, as well as shuttle bus service to transport people from the station to the grounds of the Washington Monument.

While considering as many possibilities as he could for getting people in and out of Washington, Rustin and the other organizers worked on the problems of food and comfort. While most people who came would bring their own food, Rustin knew that additional food would have to be provided at low cost. Rather than work with commercial food and beverage vendors, who would want to make a profit, he called for volunteers to make simple bag lunches—sandwiches, an apple—to be sold for a nominal price, and he likewise arranged for beverages to be available.

Although it was hoped that most people would spend just the day in the District, Rustin realized that some would arrive the night before, and some would stay the following night. Many would not be able to afford hotel rooms; and those who could afford to pay for a room would have difficulty finding a place that would accept them in the nation's very segregated capital. Rustin set up a special housing committee to arrange for as many as a thousand beds in private homes. Aware that this might not be enough, he arranged with the U.S. Army to make forty thousand blankets available. Even in the hot August weather, people sleeping out in the open would need blankets.

Health and hygiene were also on Rustin's long list of needs to consider. He arranged for several thousand portable toilets to be installed along the march route and on the Mall. He arranged with the Washington, D.C., Health Department and Red Cross to set up and staff twenty-four first-aid stations along the route and on the Mall.

Security was an important consideration. While the march was supposed to be peaceful, there were all sorts of potential trouble spots. To reduce the possibility of confrontation, Rustin asked that the only posters, signs, or slogans at the march be those provided by the march organizing committee. This request met with some resistance among various organizations that planned to take part in the march, among them the Communist party. But they acquiesced to that requirement.

Rustin did not want regular District police to patrol, and he certainly didn't want the U.S. Army or the National Guard involved, at least not in the immediate march area. After consultation with the White House, a plan was worked out whereby the National Guard, the U.S. Army, and the U.S. Marines would secure the perimeter of the demonstration area, and an even wider area around that, and that troops would be on call if needed. But within the 180 acres of the march area, there would be no uniformed officers carrying weapons. In Rustin's experience, the British police were very effective in controlling crowds without using weapons. He used the British police force as a model for the special March on Washington police force, which would consist of volunteers, uniformed and unarmed, but equipped with walkie-talkies.

Rustin knew that some New York police officers planned to participate in the march. At the time, New York police officers were required to carry their guns even while off duty. Rustin got that provision waived so that officers participating in the march would do so unarmed.

Communication during the march would be crucial. Rustin felt that all the march organizers needed ready access to telephones. Unfortunately, the committee did not have the money to pay for their installation. So Rustin met with officials of the local telephone company and made them understand that inadequate communication could have tragic results if the march was threatened with violence. The telephone company installed hundreds of pay telephones at its own expense.

In addition to planning for a march attended by one hundred thousand people, Rustin and the other march organizers could not forget the need to attract that many participants. Rustin relied on the civil rights organizations and unions to talk up the march among their members. But he also understood that it was important to establish a clear mission for the march and to disseminate printed material stating that mission. Two manuals were prepared and distributed. The first contained eight demands, the second ten. The ten final demands were, briefly:

1. Comprehensive and effective civil rights legislation.
2. Withholding of federal funds from all programs in which discrimination exists.
3. Desegregation of all school districts by the end of 1963.
4. Enforcement of the Fourteenth Amendment (which gives all citizens the right to vote).
5. A new executive order from the president, banning discrimination in all housing supported by federal funds.
6. Authority for the attorney general to bring suit when any constitutional right is violated.
7. A massive federal program to train and place all unemployed

workers, black and white, in meaningful and dignified jobs at decent wages.

8. A national minimum-wage act.
9. A broadened Fair Labor Standards Act to include areas of employment presently excluded.
10. A federal Fair Employment Practices Act barring discrimination in employment by all governments, employers, and unions.

The manuals also contained information about how best to participate in the march, down to "get a good night's sleep the night before." While such advice might have seemed unnecessary, Bayard Rustin had learned from experience: "If you want to organize anything, assume that everybody is absolutely stupid. And assume yourself that you're stupid."[1] Finally, having arranged all he could, Rustin could only hope that the planned-for one hundred thousand people would come, and that there would be no serious problems.

During July and as late as mid-August, there was some question that the march would be as well attended as hoped. For one thing, the executive council of the AFL-CIO refused to officially endorse the march. Publicly they voiced concern that violence might occur, angering members of Congress that the organization of unions had worked hard to cultivate; but the real reason for their lack of support was that many of the unions under the AFL-CIO umbrella were white and Southern-based and opposed the march.

During July and into mid-August, the numbers of people planning to participate in the march grew. Some affiliated unions from the AFL-CIO announced that they would participate, including local branches of the International Ladies Garment Workers Union, the Union of Electrical Workers, the Communication Workers of America, and, of course, A. Philip Randolph's Brotherhood of Sleeping Car Porters.

Many celebrities announced their intention to take part in the march. They included black singers Harry Belafonte, Mahalia Jackson, and Lena Horne, black actor Sidney Poitier, and white actors Charlton Heston and Marlon Brando. In fact there were so many that Rustin and the other march organizers decided to include them on the program. The entertainers would perform for the crowd at the Washington Monument, then the march to the Lincoln Memorial would take place, and then the civil rights and labor and religious leaders would give their speeches.

The structure of the formal program was another issue that required much planning and negotiation. All of the Top Ten would be speaking. No one wanted to follow Martin Luther King Jr. because he was such a charismatic speaker. The decision was made to have King speak last. Rustin would then read the demands of the marchers and Randolph would lead the marchers in a pledge to return to their communities and work to have the demands implemented. John Lewis, the youngest of the Top Ten and the representative of the youngest organization, SNCC, would speak first. All speakers would submit copies of the speeches they intended to give, both as a way to have printed transcripts available to the press and also to make sure that no one's remarks would offend any of the other speakers.

The participation of the celebrities, which Rustin and the other organizers played up to the media, helped attract more and more ordinary people. In fact, as march day approached, the idea of the march suddenly seemed to catch on in a big way. The telephones at march headquarters were jumping off the desks. Financial contributions, many from people who sent in just a few dollars, poured in, and Rustin and his committee and aides were kept busy answering questions, giving directions, and altering their plans to accommodate even more than one hundred thousand people.

As the projected number of marchers increased, racist organizations such as the American Nazi party realized that they should organize countermarches. This raised the possibility of potential violence, and the FBI began to keep an eye on groups that might cause trouble.

Another potential problem was posed by Malcolm X, who laughed at the March on Washington and called it the "farce on Washington." He charged that the major civil rights leaders were just "puppets" of the Kennedy administration and that the march was really a pep rally in support of the president. He arrived in Washington, D.C., in late August and announced that he would hold a press conference on the day before the march. That spelled trouble. Malcolm X was very influential among more militant segments of the black community, especially among Northern urban blacks. If he denounced the march on the eve of the event, he might succeed in persuading some people to stay away.

The civil rights leaders met with Malcolm X and asked him not to hold the planned press conference on August 27, arguing that he would be standing against the entire black community if he did. Malcolm X agreed not to hold the press conference as originally planned. He did hold a press conference during the march—and did indeed denounce it. But by timing his conference to occur after the event had already begun, he did not affect the number of participants. Indeed, his press conference was not well attended—most reporters were covering the march itself.

Bayard Rustin knew and liked Malcolm X. He understood the cynicism he represented. For many blacks, the very idea of non-violence was silly, given the amount of violence done to blacks by whites. He believed that Malcolm X was a legitimate spokesman for some segments of black people. And he respected the Muslim leader for deciding not to try to hamper the march, for compromising his own position for the good of the black community.

An eleventh-hour problem arose over the content of the speech John Lewis of SNCC was scheduled to give. After the texts of the various speeches were made available to the press, members of Attorney General Robert Kennedy's staff objected to some of the statements in the Lewis speech. The speech was the product of a committee (as were most actions of SNCC), but it did not matter who had written the objectionable lines, only that some found them objectionable. "We will march through the South, through the heart of Dixie, the way Sherman did. We shall pursue our own 'scorched earth' policy and burn Jim Crow to the ground—nonviolently. We shall crack the South into a thousand pieces and put them back together in the image of democracy" went one passage.[2] It was potentially inflammatory; it had no place in a peaceful march. Lewis defended the remarks and his right to make them. But most of the white march leaders did not want to be a part of the program if Lewis was going to deliver this speech. Meetings and negotiations continued well into the day of the march.

Rustin could not take part in these negotiations the way he might have liked. He had too many other things to do. He was busy overseeing the erecting of rest tents marked with red crosses, the stringing of lines for the speaker systems that would bring the speeches to the thousands of listeners on the Washington Mall, the placement of the seven thousand portable toilets and 21 four-faucet drinking fountains, the stockpiling of blankets, and the distribution centers for the bag lunches being made by volunteers at Riverside Church in New York City.

He also helped to organize the placement of forty television cameras at the Lincoln Memorial, which represented the largest outdoor television operation that had ever been attempted. Through new satellite technology, coverage of the march would be broadcast to Europe as well as across the United States. The networks' plan was to have continuous live coverage of the main program. It would be the most continuous coverage of a black event in such a public place.

The number of still photographers was uncountable, and radio coverage would also be international; the Voice of America would carry live radio broadcasts from the march all over the world.

As the Top Ten held their press conference, A. Philip Randolph announced, with obvious pride, that the basic goal of the march had already been won: "It has focused the attention of the country on the problems of human dignity and freedom for Negroes. It has reached the heart, mind, and conscience of America."[3] Meanwhile, his staunch and longtime aide, Bayard Rustin, was working behind the scenes to ensure that the march would be something of which Randolph would be proud.

CHAPTER NINE

THE MARCH ON WASHINGTON

Several hundred people arrived in Washington, D.C., the day prior to the march. Rustin and his organizers were ready for them, with sanitary facilities, blankets, and food. More people arrived in the hours before dawn on march day.

Among these people was a small group of young men who were followers of George Lincoln Rockwell, head of the American Nazi party. They planned to demonstrate against the march. Leaders of the American Nazi party had applied for a parade permit from Washington, D.C., officials and had been turned down. They had the right to be present at the march, but they were not allowed to make speeches, wear uniforms, or show placards. Perhaps those restrictions helped minimize the number of young American Nazis who came to demonstrate; at its peak, their number never topped seventy-five. When one of their leaders attempted to make a speech, he was arrested. The group marched in single file across the Potomac Bridge to Virginia.

There was also an early-morning telephoned bomb threat, but a search of the Washington Monument and Lincoln Memorial turned up no incendiary devices.

By around 7 A.M., perhaps one thousand people had gathered on the grassy slopes by the Washington Monument. Rustin and the others began to worry; they had expected far more people to arrive by then. Perhaps their projections of two hundred thousand people had been overambitious. But people continued to arrive by car, bus, and train. By 9:30, there were about forty thousand; by 11:00, there were close to one hundred thousand, and reports from the highways surrounding the capital said that the roads were clogged with buses and private cars.

As more and more people arrived, some of those already at the Washington Monument began to realize that being early did not ensure them a special spot at the Lincoln Memorial. And when, at around 12:45, they saw a group begin to move toward the Lincoln Memorial, they decided to start marching themselves.

This was the one development that Bayard Rustin, who believed he had thought of everything, had not anticipated. On paper and in discussion, everything had seemed so logical. At 12:45, the trade union people would position themselves in the front areas, just behind the section reserved for the congressmen. In this way, they would act as a buffer between the congressmen and the rest of the participants. But, as Rustin recalled later, "Well, people aren't so dumb. The minute they saw anybody moving, it dawned on them that these people were going to get the best seats! So they said . . . 'We're going, too!' So they start out. That was the one mistake we made."[1]

As soon as a few people stepped out onto Constitution Avenue, more people followed. Meanwhile, the Top Ten had been meeting with President Kennedy at the White House. When they arrived at the designated time at the designated point midway between the Washington Monument and the Lincoln Memorial, they discovered that the march had started without them!

Whitney Young of the National Urban League joked, "We'd better hurry up and catch up with our followers!"[2] and he and the others in the Top Ten were hustled up toward the head of the march. But seventy-four-year-old A. Philip Randolph was in no condition to hustle. The plan was that he, as the elder statesman of the civil rights movement and the man whose dream the march was, would walk alone at the head of the march. But he never made it to the front; he marched in the middle of the line of march leaders. Photographs show that he was not upset; his face was happy and peaceful. A modest man, Randolph had never wished to be in the limelight; his idea was that the march feature black people in all their dignity.

Black and white people, men and women, Jews and Gentiles, labor unionists and the unemployed, children and grandmothers marched—a quarter of a million strong. They marched peacefully, some dressed in their Sunday best, some in the denim overalls that had become the symbol of SNCC in the Southern voting-rights campaigns. They carried only the placards that had been provided by the march organizing committee, placards demanding jobs, decent housing, home rule for the District of Columbia, voting rights, first-class citizenship, the end of segregation in public schools, and effective civil rights laws.

Although the temperature was mercifully moderate—only in the mid-80s—the humidity was high, and some people needed the first aid facilities. But there were comparatively few instances of heat exhaustion, just as there were comparatively few incidents of violence or crime—a young man was arrested for breaking into the line of march and tearing a placard, another young man was arrested for throwing stones at march buses on the Baltimore-Washington Expressway.

When the marchers reached the Lincoln Memorial for the main program of the day, they filled the Washington Mall like a quarter of a million flowers in bloom on both sides of the large, central reflecting pool, and arrayed for yards and yards in front of the monument.

Just as the main speeches were about to begin, new problems arose over John Lewis's speech, which had already been altered once since controversy had erupted the day before. Walter Reuther, leader of the UAW, thought it was still too inflammatory; and the Very Reverend Patrick O'Boyle, archbishop of the Catholic diocese of Washington, threatened to walk off the platform if the speech was delivered as written. Under the Lincoln Memorial, in the staging area for the speakers, such loud shouting erupted that Bayard Rustin was certain some in the crowd would hear. He ordered that the National Anthem be played over the loudspeakers to drown out the sounds of conflict at the heart of the program. Then he appointed an emergency truce committee to find a solution. It included Randolph, King, Lewis, and the Reverend Eugene Carson Blake of the National Council of Churches. These men met in a guard station beneath the seat of Lincoln's statue while Rustin persuaded Archbishop O'Boyle to proceed with the convocation as planned, promising that he would show O'Boyle a copy of Lewis's speech in time to walk off the platform if he didn't like it.

Rustin stalled for time by asking several dignitaries to make brief remarks. But they could only stall for so long. Randolph eventually stepped to the microphones to give the first major speech of the afternoon. Randolph began, "We are gathered here in the largest demonstration in the history of this nation," and went on to speak of what the march was all about: a Fair Employment Practices Act, integrated public schools, a free democratic society. He talked about how civil rights and economic equality were intertwined. He promised that "we shall return again, and again, to Washington in ever-growing numbers until total freedom is ours."

After a speech by the Reverend Eugene Carson Blake, there was a moment to honor six women of the civil rights movement who had been conspicuously absent until then. They included Rosa Parks, who had sparked the Montgomery bus boycott; Diane Nash Bevel, who had sent Nashville students to take up the Freedom Ride when the first riders had been arrested; Daisy Bates, who had helped found SNCC and helped the first black students to integrate Central High School in Little Rock, Arkansas; and Gloria Richardson, who had formed the Cambridge Nonviolent Action Committee earlier in the year to force integration of public facilities. Also included were two women who had lost their husbands to the cause: Myrlie Evers, whose husband, Medgar, had recently been assassinated in Jackson, Mississippi; and Mrs. Herbert Lee, whose husband had been assassinated by white segregationists in McComb, Mississippi, in 1961, because of his attempts to get blacks to register to vote.

Then John Lewis stepped to the microphones. He was greeted by a roar of applause from those who realized that he had suffered much physical pain and many arrests in the cause. Thanks to the frantic last-minute rewriting by the committee appointed by Rustin, his speech had been toned down enough so that Archbishop O'Boyle did not make good on his threat to walk off the platform. The objectionable lines now came out as: "We will march through the South, through the streets of Jackson, through the streets of Danville, through the streets of Cambridge, through the streets of Birmingham . . . But we will march with the spirit of love and with the spirit of dignity that we have shown here today."

Lewis was followed at the microphones by Walter Reuther, president of the UAW. James Farmer of CORE was to have spoken next; but he was in jail in Louisiana, where he had been arrested for leading a demonstration. Floyd B. McKissick, national chairman of CORE, read a letter from Farmer. Musical selections and a prayer followed; then Whitney Young of the National Urban League, Mathew Ahmann of the National Catholic Conference for Interracial Justice, and Roy Wilkins of the NAACP were featured. Mahalia Jackson sang the spiritual "I Been 'Buked and I Been Scorned," and Rabbi Joachim Prinz of the American Jewish Congress gave a speech.

By this time the crowd was beginning to grow restless. Then Martin Luther King Jr. stepped to the microphones, and there was a stir of anticipation. King was well known as an emotional and inspiring speaker. However, the size of the crowd, the presence of national and world press, and the historic nature of the event may have caused him to begin his remarks in an unemotional tone. He read from his prepared script and did not sound like a Baptist preacher. But when King reached the part of his speech in which he said, "We will not be satisfied until justice rolls down like waters and righteousness like a mighty stream," his voice rose and fell in preaching cadences, and when the crowd responded, he departed from his prepared and approved text. Inspired by the event and by the reaction of the crowd, he gave forth words that would become famous:

> *I have a dream . . . deeply rooted in the American dream . . .*
> *I have a dream my four little children will one day live in a nation*
> *where they will not be judged by the color of their skin but by the*
> *content of their character. I have a dream today!*

He continued to talk about his dream. When he finished, the crowd roared with cheers, and Bayard Rustin had to wait several minutes for calm to be restored before he could read the list of marchers' demands. After A. Philip Randolph delivered the pledge of the marchers to return to their communities and work to secure those demands, Rustin joyfully led the crowd in responding to that pledge.

As five o'clock arrived, the crowd began to leave. Everything was right on schedule. One of the leaders turned to Rustin and said, "Rustin, I have to hand it to you. You're a genius."[3]

The leaders then departed for a special prearranged meeting with President Kennedy. The success of the march had far surpassed even their most ambitious hopes, and they wasted no time in using the power the march had given them to push for the strongest civil rights bills possible. While they were meeting with the president, and later with reporters, Bayard Rustin was already seeing to the cleanup. He had planned carefully for the march's aftermath; almost immediately workers began to sweep up the debris and remove tons of trash. Portable toilets and drinking fountains were packed up; microphones and loudspeaker wires were unstrung from trees; chairs were removed; and the makeshift podium in front of the Lincoln Memorial was broken down. Personal belongings found on the Mall were placed in a March on Washington lost and found.

On the promotion side, Rustin oversaw the production of press releases about the success of the march. There were many newspaper articles extolling the march from which the press releases could quote, like the following from an article by Claude Sitton for the *New York Times*: "Few who saw the marchers or talked with their leaders could be but impressed by their enthusiasm, determination and confidence. Few could but ask if the seeming resignation with which many Negroes once accepted their place in American society had disappeared forever . . . Today's appeal to Congress and the nation, more than anything else, served notice that the Negro believes that he is as much a master of his destiny as any American."[4]

And there were the remarks from the president of the United States to quote as well: "The cause of twenty million Negroes has been advanced by the program conducted so appropriately before the nation's shrine to the Great Emancipator, but even more significant is the contribution to all mankind."

A. Philip Randolph and Bayard Rustin had envisioned the March on Washington for Jobs and Freedom as a climax of the direct-action civil rights movement; later events proved how right they were. Never again would so many people be of such like mind and so determined to demonstrate peacefully for what they believed. Bayard Rustin, as chief organizer, had given them the opportunity to do so. Forever after, Rustin spoke of the March on Washington as his proudest moment. He once remarked that he liked to "stare at it" because "it was one of my most beautiful periods of work in my life."[5]

CHAPTER TEN

INTERNATIONAL ORGANIZER

Many in the nation remained unconvinced of the right of African Americans to full equality. The South continued to resist the end of segregation. On the first day of school that fall in Birmingham, Alabama, state governor George Wallace sent Alabama National Guardsmen to prevent three public schools from complying with court-ordered integration. The following Sunday, the all-black Sixteenth Street Baptist Church in Birmingham was bombed, killing four young girls.

Two months later, on November 22, President Kennedy was assassinated while riding in a motorcade in Dallas, Texas. There had been death threats against the president before he went to Dallas, but he had declined his advisers' recommendation that he travel in a limousine equipped with a protective bullet-proof bubble. Kennedy's assassin, Lee Harvey Oswald, was a troubled man with ties to Cuba and resentment over Kennedy's earlier Bay of Pigs invasion of Cuba. Whether Kennedy's stand on racial equality had any direct influence on his killing is not known.

Vice President Lyndon B. Johnson, sworn in as president after Kennedy's death, vowed to press on with the late president's civil rights legislation. On July 2, 1964, he signed into law the Civil Rights Act of 1964, the most sweeping civil rights legislation in a century. It was followed the next year by the Voting Rights Act of 1965. These two pieces of legislation put into place the legal basis for the end of segregation; the civil rights battle in the South shifted to the courts.

Bayard Rustin had always believed that the key to racial equality was equality of economic opportunity, and in the Johnson administration he was able to put some of his ideas into practice. Rustin operated several programs authorized under President Johnson's "Great Society" umbrella, including the Joint Apprenticeship Program, the Youth Employment Program, and the Recruitment and Training Program (RTP, Inc.), all of which aimed to give young African Americans the skills and experience needed to find and keep jobs.

In the meantime, Malcolm X left the Nation of Islam and softened his antiwhite stand. Following his first pilgrimage to Mecca in Saudi Arabia, which every true Muslim must undertake at least once in his lifetime, Malcom X discovered that worldwide Islam included whites as well as blacks. He concluded that the problem in the United States was not racism so much as it was an unjust economic and social system. He returned with a vastly different philosophy of race relations and founded a new Organization of Afro-American Unity that would work with whites for better race relations. Soon after, in February 1965, he was assassinated by members of the Nation of Islam.

The following year, more militant factions in SNCC took control of that organization. They let former white members and supporters know they were no longer welcome and announced a new campaign: "Black Power!"

The stage of the civil rights campaign shifted to the North. There, segregation existed, too; but it was harder to fight. The segregation wasn't grounded in laws, but was just as entrenched in housing patterns and custom. Martin Luther King Jr. and the SCLC, seeing that the framework had been built for legal equality in the South, tried to use the same tactics of nonviolent protest in Chicago. They found little support. Northern urban blacks responded to militancy, not to nonviolence.

Nevertheless, King's efforts in the successful nonviolent civil rights campaign could never be overshadowed, and in 1964 he was awarded the Nobel Peace Prize, the youngest man ever to be so honored. Bayard Rustin, who had continued to advise King, accompanied King to Oslo, Norway, to accept the prize.

Now a world-renowned spokesman for peace, King saw his role as a broader one. He stepped away from the civil rights sphere and spoke out against the United States's involvement in North Vietnam—and was roundly criticized. He was not deterred. He believed that he should speak out for nonviolence in any unequal or violent situation.

In early 1968, King was asked by striking black sanitation workers in Memphis, Tennessee, to visit their city and show support for their demands of equal pay and working conditions with their white coworkers. King went to Memphis with some reluctance, not only because of his busy schedule but also because of a strong sense of danger to his own life. He participated in one of the sanitation workers' marches in Memphis and was appalled to see it degenerate into violence, mostly because of young black marchers who broke rank and started beating up people. Aware that the nonviolent civil rights movement—not to mention his own reputation as its leader—might suffer because of that eruption of violence, King made plans for a second, peaceful march.

King did not live to see the second march take place. On the evening of April 4, 1968, he was assassinated on the balcony of the Lorraine Motel in Memphis.

Amid their grief over the untimely death of their husband and friend, King's widow, Coretta Scott King, and his best friend and associate, the Reverend Ralph David Abernathy, understood that they must carry on his campaign for peace. They decided to continue with plans for that second march, as a tribute to King, and they called on Bayard Rustin's organizational skills to ensure that the second march would do honor to King's memory.

Rustin was on a commercial airline flight bound for Memphis when his flight was diverted to an air force base outside Washington, D.C., on orders of President Lyndon B. Johnson (who assumed such powers in times of national emergency). Johnson had also diverted the planes on which other civil rights leaders were traveling so that as many people as possible could meet with him at the White House to discuss prevention of full-scale rioting.

Rustin told the president that in his opinion the most positive thing he himself could do was to continue on to Memphis as promised and to honor King's memory by seeing to it that the peaceful march King had wanted took place. The president agreed and ordered a government plane to fly Rustin to Memphis. "As I was leaving in this government plane," Rustin recalled, "I saw the first flames and smoke circling Washington and coming out of Sixteenth Street, and K Street, where the rioting had begun."[1]

Rustin missed the funeral of King in Atlanta because he had promised to oversee the second, nonviolent march. "Mrs. King and [Harry] Belafonte left Atlanta, came to the march, and left an hour or so later, again on a government plane, to get back for King's funeral; but I had to stay in Memphis, to clear things up."[2]

The death of Martin Luther King Jr. signaled the end of the civil rights era in American history, although it was certainly not the end of civil rights work.

Rustin remained involved in the movement. He was elected chairman of the executive committee of the Leadership Conference on Civil Rights, a group of civil rights leaders who met periodically to discuss and plan overall strategy. In the year of King's death he began to receive recognition for his work in the form of honorary degrees given by colleges and universities. In June 1968 he received such degrees from both Montclair State College in New Jersey and the New School for Social Research in New York City. In ensuing years, he would receive honorary doctorates from Harvard, Yale, and Brandeis universities and Haverford College. The awarding of the degrees was a recognition of the major contributions he had made to the nonviolent civil rights movement. The fact that Rustin was given these honorary degrees may have signaled a liberalization of attitudes, at least in the northeastern United States, toward gay people. By the time of his death, Rustin had received a total of eighteen honorary degrees, primarily from colleges and universities in the northeastern United States.

Rustin became more active in the international sphere. During the administration of President Richard M. Nixon (1968–1974), but long before the president decided to publicly and formally pursue friendly relations with the former U.S. enemy mainland China, Rustin was a founding member of the National Committee on United States–China Relations. One of its initiatives was to bring a group of Chinese Ping-Pong players and jugglers to the United States. "We didn't get a penny from the State Department," Rustin recalled, "[but] the State Department was very anxious for us to set up the committee because they wanted some means by which they could measure Americans' response to the Chinese people, in this country."[3] As a result of the committee's work, some of its members were invited to visit China.

Rustin was vice-president-international, along with Swedish actress Liv Ullmann, of the International Rescue Committee. The committee concerns itself with, among other issues, the plight of refugees around the world. He was part of an international leadership contingent for the March for Survival to the Cambodian border, protesting the treatment of refugees by the Khmer Rouge (the ruling power in that country), and attempting to deliver much needed food and medical supplies to the refugees. In early 1987 he toured refugee camps in Thailand.

Rustin was also very involved in the Vietnamese "boat people" situation. The boat people sought escape from their hard lives in Vietnam by sailing, or sometimes simply drifting, in boats of all sizes across the South China Sea to Thailand. Rustin wrote articles, testified in Congress in an effort to secure aid for the refugees, and visited the refugee camps several times.

In 1985, Rustin explained the myriad activities he had undertaken for the International Rescue Committee: "It is my duty to go annually to such places as Thailand—where we have refugee camps, where we run medical and education [programs] for refugees—Pakistan, where we run them for the Afghanis—Europe, where we help the people who are fleeing from the crackdown on *Solidarnosc* in Poland—Europe, where we have efforts going on attempting to put pressure to get Jewish refugees out of Russia—Latin America, India . . . Now, I just got back from Botswana, Lesotho, and Swaziland, where I presented to the International Rescue Committee a plan for the education and medical care of South African refugees' children from age twelve to seventeen who are being driven out for a variety of reasons."[4]

Rustin continued to be active in antiapartheid work. He visited South Africa in 1983 and 1984 and set up a group called Project South Africa to support nongovernmental groups working to build democracy there. At one point in the 1980s he was denied a visa by the disapproving South African government, so his assistant went in his place.

During his frequent travels, Rustin began to collect art and artifacts. Some came as gifts from dealers who had asked him to look for items abroad that they could sell. They trusted his taste. The sale of his antique musical instrument collection also provided funds for these new purchases. He had decided to sell that collection for a variety of reasons. First of all, it took up every available inch of space in his apartment. In addition, Rustin was concerned about the safety of his collection. While living on West 107th Street on the Upper West Side of Manhattan, he had suffered two burglaries. After moving to an apartment in the downtown section of Manhattan called Chelsea, he had been robbed again. This last robbery had been at gunpoint, and the thief had taken a watch that had belonged to Rustin's grandfather, one of the few mementos in his possession of the older man. Rustin's realization that antiques must be stored in climate-controlled environments, which he could not provide, was still another reason he decided to sell the collection. And, finally, his interests had changed. As he once explained, "I think that people often collect one thing at one time of their lives, have an intensive experience until it exhausts itself, and then go on to something else. The things I [collect] have changed and they change me, and as I changed so do the works."[5]

Rustin was now far more likely to fancy an elaborately carved walking stick from Africa, an incense burner from India, or a sculpture of a Madonna and child. Having sold his instrument collection, he began to collect eclectic items from around the world.

His collection of walking sticks grew quickly, and he was in the habit of carrying a walking stick whenever he went out. One Sunday in January 1972, he went walking in Times Square with a married couple who were friends of his, and decided to carry a cane that happened to have a sword concealed in it. He was arrested for carrying a dangerous weapon! News of the arrest of the man who had spent his life as a conscientious objector and a worker for nonviolent causes made headlines. When police saw that Rustin had a collection of thirty to forty walking sticks and canes, they dropped the charges.

Another major part of Rustin's collection was images of the Madonna and child—carved in wood, sculptured in stone, painted on canvas. Some people wondered if this interest of Rustin's was related to the fact that he had missed that important relationship in his own early life.

While he may not have had a close relationship with his biological parents as a child, Rustin had felt loved and wanted by his grandparents. He had also maintained close ties with his relatives who lived in New York—his aunt, Bessie LeBon, and one of her sons. He'd also had a unique and long-lasting relationship as an adult with a mentor. By the 1960s, he had been working closely with A. Philip Randolph for some thirty years; and the relationship continued. In 1964, shortly before Randolph retired from his position with the AFL-CIO, Rustin had helped to found and had become cochairman of the A. Philip Randolph Institute. Officially, its purpose was to promote basic changes in the social and economic structure of the United States through political action programs and a broad-based national coalition of minorities, working people, and the poor.

In fact, the main reason for founding the institute, according to Rustin, was to give him a base. "Randolph had always felt that I should have some kind of agency through which to work," Rustin once explained. "But he also felt that my strength was with new ideas, and while he felt I should have some kind of an institution to work with, he did not want me to be institutionalized."[6] Over the years, the NAACP, the Urban League, the SCLC, and other civil rights organizations had all asked Rustin to take jobs with them. But Randolph had always advised against Rustin's getting tied to an institution with an already-established program. He believed that he and Rustin had started many initiatives over the years that others followed but would probably not have started themselves.

Instead, Randolph decided, "We'll have to create something for Bayard," and together the two old friends began to plan the A. Philip Randolph Institute.

They invited the leaders of the major civil rights organizations to be advisers. The leaders agreed, with the understanding that the A. Philip Randolph Institute would not be a membership organization and thus in direct competition with their own organizations. Rustin had misgivings about going along with their wishes; without a membership, the institute would not be able to engage in fund-raising appeals. "How are we going to live?" he asked Randolph. Randolph answered, "By your imagination."[7]

The primary funding for the institute came from unions, especially the AFL-CIO. Its first headquarters was on 125th Street in Harlem; in 1969, it moved downtown to the building that housed the United Federation of Teachers, the New York City local of the American Federation of Teachers.

The A. Philip Randolph Institute served the existing civil rights groups by producing educational materials, such as pamphlets and conference programs, for them to use. A major emphasis, however, was in the economic sphere, especially with labor unions, which both Randolph and Rustin believed must play a pivotal role in the alliance they wished to foster.

Rustin believed very firmly in democracy and its promotion all over the world, and so there was also a strong core of democracy and internationalism in the work of the institute. For example, the institute conducted "get out the vote" campaigns at election time, calling potential voters to remind them to cast their ballots and even providing an A. Philip Randolph Institute "courtesy car" to ferry voters to the polls.

And the institute was very active on the international stage, primarily because of Rustin's belief that "You can have a democracy and things are bad. But there is no way you can improve things without a democracy."[8] In the early 1970s Rustin formed a group called Black Americans in Support of Israel. This was a time when many African Americans sided with the Arab nations in the Middle East conflict, despite Israel's history of providing training and technical assistance to developing African nations. Asked in an interview why he had pushed for the formation of the new group, Rustin responded that he had done so "for the same reason I have been working on behalf of the Vietnamese boat people, the same reason I have been helping the Haitian boat people emigrating to this country, for the same reason I have traveled to Africa to fight for the independence movement there.

"Democracy is the key to the elimination of segregation and discrimination. So whenever democracy is in trouble, and where people are mistreated, it is my obligation to do something about it." Israel, he went on to point out, was the only democracy in the Middle East. It also had a free trade-union movement. "It is not because they are Jews," he added.[9]

Together, Rustin and Randolph were on the first committee in support of a national holiday for Martin Luther King Jr.'s birthday. Rustin liked to point out that it was a Harlem resident named Howard Bennett who started that first committee, and that only after Bennett began to make some headway did the Urban League, the NAACP, Mrs. King, and others join the effort seriously.

A. Philip Randolph died on May 16, 1979. Many regarded Randolph as the most important African American leader of the century, even more influential than W. E. B. Du Bois and Martin Luther King Jr. While the death of the man who had been his friend and mentor for nearly half a century was a difficult blow for Rustin, in some ways it may have freed Rustin to speak for himself. Not long after the death of his mentor, Rustin told an interviewer, "I would not put on another March on Washington if you begged me. You can solve moral problems by marching. You cannot solve economic problems by marching."[10] He might not have said that had Randolph still been alive, for the late labor leader's life had been strongly devoted to such demonstrations.

In the last years of his own life, however, Rustin referred to the March on Washington as his proudest moment. There is really no contradiction in his statements: the efforts that he and Randolph made had been right for their time.

Rustin maintained a keen interest in economic and social events in the United States. He met and counseled the new leaders who arose in the African American community, from Jesse Jackson to Benjamin Hooks of the NAACP. He kept current with international affairs. He was sought out by leaders and thinkers the world over for his ideas. In January 1987 he was affiliated with no fewer than thirty organizations, from Actor's Equity to the League for Industrial Democracy, from the National Coalition for Haitian Refugees to Democracy International, from the United States Holocaust Memorial Council to the Washington Institute for Near East Policy.

On March 17, 1987, hundreds of friends and acquaintances attended a special seventy-fifth birthday party for Rustin. He died five months later, on August 24. He had just returned from a trip to Haiti, where he had met with democratic forces emerging after the downfall of the Duvalier dictatorship. Over one thousand people attended the memorial service at Manhattan's Community Church on October 1. They were civil rights, political, religious, labor, and humanitarian leaders; they were also plain people whose lives he had touched in some way. Many of them spoke about what knowing Rustin had meant to them. Vernon Jordan, former head of the National Urban League, called him a "consummate adviser" and the "intellectual bank" of the civil rights movement. Lane Kirkland, president of the AFL-CIO, told the crowd, "He understood and taught that there are no black issues, no women's issues, no labor issues that are not a part of the same struggle for human justice." John Lewis, once the leader of SNCC and now a congressman from Georgia, said that Rustin was "totally committed to the building of an international democracy."

When the speeches were over, the crowd sat in silence as a tape was played of Rustin singing the spiritual "Nobody Knows the Trouble I've Seen." Many wept, remembering that Bayard Rustin had indeed seen trouble—in his own life as well as in the life of the world in which he had lived for seventy-five years. But he never gave up hoping that things would get better, and he never stopped working to make his hopes a reality.

Notes

Chapter 1. "Growing Up Quaker"

1. "The Reminiscences of Bayard Rustin," Columbia University Oral History Project, interview with Ed Edwin, November 14, 1984, p. 2.
2. Ibid., p. 3.
3. Ibid., p. 6.
4. Ibid., p. 13.
5. Ibid., p. 14.
6. Ibid., p. 13.
7. Ibid., p. 6.
8. *Op. cit.*
9. Ibid., p. 7.
10. Ibid., p. 1.
11. *Op. cit.*
12. Ibid, pp. 22–23.
13. Ibid., p. 9.
14. Ibid., p. 12.
15. Ibid., pp. 22–23.

Chapter 2. "College and Communism"

1. "An Interview with Bayard Rustin," *Open Hands* (no date), p.4. Bayard Rustin Papers, Bayard Rustin Institute.
2. George Chauncey Jr. and Lisa Kennedy, "Time on Two Crosses: An Interview with Bayard Rustin," *Gay Life* (1987), no page. Bayard Rustin Papers, Bayard Rustin Institute.
3. *Open Hands*, p. 4.
4. "Reminiscences," November 14, 1984, p. 32.
5. Ibid., pp. 32–33.
6. "Reminiscences," January 24, 1985, p. 67.

7. Ibid., p. 63.
8. "Reminiscences," February 28, 1985, p. 81.
9. "Reminiscences," January 24, 1985, p. 65.
10. Ibid., pp. 66–67.
11. "Reminiscences," November 14, 1984, p. 29.

Chapter 3. "Conscientious Objector"

1. "Reminiscences," January 24, 1985, p. 70.
2. James Farmer, *Lay Bare the Heart*, p. 109.
3. "Reminiscences," January 24, 1985, p. 74.
4. Ibid., p. 70.
5. Ibid., p. 72.
6. "Reminiscences," February 28, 1985, p. 80.
7. "Reminiscences," January 24, 1985, p. 74.
8. Ibid., p. 75.
9. "Reminiscences," September 12, 1985, p. 326.

Chapter 4. "Greater Militancy"

1. Bayard Rustin, "We Challenged Jim Crow," *Down the Line*, p. 22.
2. Farmer, p. 300.
3. Ibid., p. 292.
4. "Reminiscences," February 28, 1985, p. 84.
5. Ibid., pp. 82–84.
6. "Reminiscences," September 12, 1985, p. 295.
7. "Reminiscences," February 28, 1985, pp. 84–85.

Chapter 5. "The Civil Rights Movement Begins"

1. *Open Hands*, p. 5.
2. *Op. cit.*
3. *Op. cit.*
4. "Reminiscences," April 3, 1985, p. 135.
5. Ibid., p. 136.
6. Ibid., p. 138.

Chapter 6. "The Southern Christian Leadership Conference"

1. "Reminiscences," February 28, 1985, pp. 120–22.
2. *Op. cit.*
3. "Reminiscences," April 3, 1985, p. 154.
4. Ibid., p. 161.
5. "Reminiscences," May 30, 1985, p. 268.

Chapter 7. "To March or Not to March"

1. Taylor Branch, *Parting the Waters*, p. 873.
2. Ibid., p. 853.
3. "Reminiscences," May 8, 1985, p. 209.

Chapter 8. "March Organizer"

1. Branch, p. 873.
2. Ibid., p. 874.
3. Ibid., p. 879.

Chapter 9. "The March on Washington"

1. "Reminiscences," May 8, 1985, p. 237.
2. Jim Haskins, *The March on Washington*, p. 109.
3. Ibid.
4. The *New York Times* (July 13, 1963), p. 1.
5. "Reminiscences," September 12, 1985, p. 321.

Chapter 10. "International Organizer"

1. "Reminiscences," April 3, 1985, p. 187.
2. *Op. cit.*
3. "Reminiscences," May 30, 1985, p. 280.
4. "Reminiscences," November 6, 1985, p. 360.
5. Susan Ginsburg, "Bayard Rustin, Portrait as a Collector," *Auction* (May 1970), p. 40.
6. "Reminiscences," May 8, 1985, p. 213.
7. Ibid., p. 214.
8. Ibid., p. 215.
9. *The News World* (February 10, 1980), p. 7A. Bayard Rustin Papers, Bayard Rustin Institute.
10. *Op. cit.*

Bibliography

Books

Branch, Taylor. *Parting the Waters: America in the King Years 1954–1963.* New York: Simon & Schuster, 1988.

Farmer, James. *Lay Bare the Heart: An Autobiography of the Civil Rights Movement.* New York: Arbor House, 1985.

Garrow, David J. *Bearing the Cross: Martin Luther King, Jr., and the Southern Christian Leadership Conference.* New York: William Morrow & Co., 1986.

Haskins, James. *Freedom Rides.* New York: Hyperion Books for Children, 1995.

———. *The March on Washington.* New York: HarperCollins Publishers, 1993.

Rustin, Bayard. *Down the Line: The Collected Writings of Bayard Rustin.* Chicago: Quadrangle Books, 1971.

Williams, Juan. *Eyes on the Prize: America's Civil Rights Years, 1954–1965.* New York: Viking Press, 1987.

Other Sources

Bayard Rustin Papers. Bayard Rustin Fund, Inc., New York.

Columbia University Oral History Project. "The Reminiscences of Bayard Rustin." Fourteen interviews with Bayard Rustin. November 14, 1984, through June 18, 1987.

Ginsburg, Susan. "Bayard Rustin, Portrait as a Collector." *Auction* (May 1970): 40.

Index